PAWSITIVELY IN LOVE AGAIN AT CHRISTMAS

CHRISTMAS IN SNOWY FALLS BOOK 1

JACQUELINE WINTERS

Copy Editor: Write Girl Editing Services

Cover Design: Blue Valley Author Services

Proofreading: FictionEdit.com

CHAPTER 1

$\mathscr{N}$OAH

NOAH TAGGERT PULLED into the driveway of his parents' two-story home, surprised to find the usual pack of cars missing. A lack of tire tracks marring the fresh, puffy snow caused an eyebrow to raise.

Cutting the engine, he popped out of the rented truck before one of a dozen excuses to drive away took hold. He hadn't warned his parents or any of his siblings that he was making a quick trip home to Snowy Falls. Mom would've only fussed, packing his already tight schedule with family activities. If all went smoothly, he'd be on a plane back to Montana tomorrow. There just wasn't time for gingerbread houses and Christmas carols.

Besides, the shorter his stay, the better his odds of avoiding Everly Jensen. The thought of seeing her, happy with another man, made his stomach tie in knots.

Suitcase retrieved from the back seat, he trudged through the snow. With Dad retired, the un-shoveled walk didn't make much sense either. If the Christmas tree lights hadn't been twinkling through the living room window, Noah might've thought the place abandoned.

Four years had gone by since he last stood before the red-sided, white-trimmed home. Four years since he heard Cole and Blakely fighting over the last drumstick after Dad claimed his. Four years since he pulled the canned peaches down from the top shelf when Mom couldn't reach them. Four years . . .

Noah drew a breath, shaking his memories free and returning to the present. He'd learned how to do that on Uncle Arthur's ranch. Live in the moment, or your last failure could cost you another. Life on the ranch as the head veterinarian had consumed Noah's life since he left, and he let it. Wasn't hard. Each day was more rewarding than the last, even the hard, sleepless ones. Didn't mean that Mom wasn't going to give him an earful for missing so many family holidays.

If she's home.

He stepped beneath the covered patio, shaking his cowboy hat free of fresh snowflakes. A snowdrift against the far pillar covered most of a stone pattern that comprised its lower half, boxing him in and urging him toward the front door. He reached for the knob, admiring a massive wreath decorated in red ribbon and gold ornaments that adorned the front door. No doubt one of Mom's creations. For a reason he couldn't pinpoint, the wreath gave him pause. *Probably the lecture that's waiting inside.*

Instead of barging in, he rang the doorbell and waited for the shuffle of approaching footsteps or the chorus of voices arguing over who would answer the door. But he heard neither.

Noah rang the bell again, then tried the knob. *Locked?*

It was only five days until Christmas. Mom was typically on lockdown mode by this time, frantically baking, decorating, and finding new daily hiding spots for presents. Though his siblings were all adults, Mom always had someone at her disposal this time of year to run last-minute errands.

When Noah's hunt for the spare key turned up empty, he pulled his phone from a coat pocket and searched for Mom's number. He braced for the shock, then scolding, that would accompany the surprise news he dropped on her. But after two rings, her call went to voicemail.

Fingers stiffening from cold, he hurried back to his truck and started the heater. "Where is everyone?"

The Taggert household was a bustling zoo around the holidays. No matter what was happening in town—outside of the Christmas Eve tree lighting ceremony, of course—there was always *someone* here. He refused to believe that tradition had changed in the past four years.

Noah sent a text to his brother Cole, staring at his phone as the message struggled to send. After two minutes, a *failure to send* error popped up. "Really?"

Living on a remote ranch in Montana with no cell service and unreliable Internet did keep Noah out of the loop on a lot of family matters. But surely someone would've sent him an invite—or at least an email—if the entire family decided to skip town for Christmas. Maybe Grandma Annie could make sense of this. He'd driven by her house on his way over here and saw the lights on.

Weaving through the residential neighborhood, Noah took in the familiar sights. Snowmen in front yards, kids playing under a thick layer of snow gear, and the twinkle of lights from houses that never shut them off after Thanksgiving. He loved the openness of Montana, but he missed the charm of small-town Maine. Even if reminders of Everly were sprinkled on every corner.

From Grandma Annie's front porch, Noah heard Christmas music playing inside. Maybe the family had piled into one vehicle to join the party. He rapped on the front door, announcing his arrival, and then let himself in.

"Grandma Annie?" he called, stepping inside and kicking off his snow-covered boots by the door. "Anyone home?"

He shrugged out of his coat and hat, leaving them on a hook as he drew in a deep, appreciative breath.

Following the savory aroma of homemade soup, Noah passed through the empty living room on his way to the kitchen, confused at the scattered boxes of ornaments and decorations strewn all over. *No tree yet?* "Grandma Annie?" he called again, certain the music had muffled his arrival.

"In here." She emerged from the pantry carrying a stack of plastic bowls, no doubt for the soup. When she finally turned to see him, she let out a startled squeak. Bowls and lids scattered into the air. "Noah Taggert, is that really you?"

He rolled his eyes, ensuring she spotted the exaggeration he used. "I've only been gone four years. Not forty." After collecting the lids and handing them over, he wrapped her in a bear hug.

"Oh, it's *good* to see you!" She rocked him from side to side before she let him go. "I didn't know you were coming. Your mom—"

"I didn't tell anyone." Having to make the confession filled him with guilt. Though Mom and Dad always hosted Christmas Day, Grandma Annie held tight to her Christmas Eve traditions. He hated to break her heart and admit he wouldn't be in town long enough to enjoy her pumpkin pie. But the less opportunity Mom had to convince him to stick around, the better his odds were of avoiding Everly. "I wanted it to be a surprise."

"You don't know."

Noah's smile dropped as he leaned against the counter, unsettled by the ominous tone in her voice. Surely if someone had been hurt—or worse—his family would've found a way to notify him. Spotty Internet on the ranch still allowed him to check emails a couple of times a week. "Know what?"

"They're all gone."

"Gone?"

"Why don't you make yourself comfortable." Grandma Annie pointed at the round table tucked in the nook. "I'll fix you some coffee. Sorry I don't have the cookies baked yet. That's on tomorrow's list, you see."

Noah dropped into a chair, his back aimed mostly toward the window, and waited. Seconds pounded away like minutes as every worst-case scenario he could imagine rolled through his mind. Had someone been hurt, or in an accident? Was someone sick?

From the corner of his eye, Noah caught a blur of yellow zipping through the backyard, but he wasn't quick enough to make out what it was.

"Guess you don't get *all* the news living out on that ranch in the middle of nowhere," Grandma Annie said, sliding him a cup of coffee with a submerged candy cane leaning against the rim.

The peppermint aroma called to him, momentarily distracting him from whatever news he hadn't received. He hadn't had anything fancier than black coffee for longer than he could remember. Coffee with a hint of peppermint was a guilty pleasure he sorely missed.

Grandma arched a brow, plainly dragging out the tension. "Your mom didn't leave you a voicemail? Or maybe Chloe?"

Noah sat up straighter, pushing nostalgia aside. "Grandma, you're worrying me. Is someone hurt?"

"Oh, no, nothing like that." Her chipper tone lifted the gloom swimming in his chest. "It's Blakley. You probably didn't know she was dating that hotshot lawyer from New York."

Chloe—the sister who told him everything in broken-dam fashion in her lengthy emails—had mentioned something about a whirlwind romance no one expected to last. Blakely was the most impulsive of the Taggert siblings, and the note about this hadn't raised any red flags. "Chloe mentioned it," he said, taking a slow sip.

"She ran off to Cancun. To *elope!*"

Noah nearly spit out his coffee. "She what?"

"Second your family heard that, they headed

straight for the airport to stop the wedding. Chloe's the only one still in town, but not for long. She has a rescue dog to pick up in Bangor and no one else could go. She'll be on the road any minute now."

Noah's heart pounded in his ears. He needed his family to be *here* or he couldn't fulfill Uncle Arthur's final wish. "When are they coming back?"

Grandma Annie stirred the candy cane in her coffee before lifting it to her lips. "Don't know. Whenever they can talk Blakley off the ledge, I guess. I just hope they're back before the big snowstorm headed our way or they might miss Christmas. Wouldn't that be a shame?"

Noah hid his panic behind his coffee mug, sipping slowly as everything sank in. Uncle Arthur had passed away six months ago, refusing a big, flashy memorial service. He didn't want anyone flying halfway across the country to pay their last respects. But he did ask Noah to scatter some of his ashes in his hometown of Snowy Falls. His one stipulation was that Noah's parents and his siblings be present. *All* of his siblings.

What if they couldn't talk Blakely out of it? What if she didn't elope but decided to stay in Cancun for a couple of weeks? What if— Noah shook it off, clearing his throat with a reminder of a present need. "Did Mom leave you a spare key for the house?" he asked, realizing he'd be stuck in town an extra day or two. *Hopefully no more than that.*

"You're not going to stay there, are you?"

He slid out of his chair and carried his empty mug to the sink. "That was my plan."

"I have plenty of room," Grandma Annie insisted. She met him at the sink, rinsing out her mug. "I'd love the company, Noah. And to hear all about life on the ranch. I haven't talked to you in ages, you know."

Grandma Annie's guilt trip did its job. "Okay, I'll stay here."

"Wonderful." She squeezed him in a side hug. "It's so great to have you home for Christmas. About the best gift I could ask for. Aside from your family saving your sister from making a huge mistake, that is." In a mumble, she added, "I don't know what got into Blakley."

"I better grab my suitcase." Noah slipped on his boots and hat, but rushed outside without his coat. Two feet from his truck, he saw the yellow blur again. Only this time, the dog stopped at the edge of the driveway.

"Who do you belong to?" he asked, as if the dog might answer. But he didn't see anyone running toward the house to retrieve the yellow lab.

The dog barked at him a few times, tail wagging furiously. The lab's collar jingled when the dog leaned forward, butt wiggling in a playful stance. He looked through the house windows, hoping to spot Grandma Annie. Maybe she'd know who the dog belonged to and point him to the right house.

"Come here, boy," he said in his sweetest voice. Being a vet, he liked to think he was good with animals. But his specialty was horses, not dogs. When Noah took a step closer, the lab sprang to his feet and raced around the side of the house.

When Noah didn't immediately trek into the deep snow, the dog ran back.

"Okay, okay. I get it. You want me to follow you. Coming, Lassie."

Noah was so focused on where each booted step landed in the deep snow that he didn't notice the ladder until the dog barked again. Perched near the top with Christmas lights extended toward the eave of Grandma Annie's house was the only woman he'd ever truly loved: Everly Jensen.

$\mathcal{E}$VERLY

Everly clamped her gloved hands around the ladder's metal rungs and took a deep breath. "I can do this." She repeated the pep talk to herself each time she moved the ladder, repositioning to string the next few feet of lights.

Except, this time, the mantra had zero effect. Her boots refused to lift from the snow-covered ground. Bending her forehead to the icy, metal rung, she closed her eyes for a moment. "Come on. I can do this."

Behind her, oblivious to Everly's mild panic attack, Kenobi zipped around in the yard. When it came to snow, the yellow lab conveniently forgot he was a seven-year-old rescue and his puppy side came to life. Her dog's excitement was the newest reason she loved winter in Maine.

Kenobi let out a deep bark.

"Okay, okay. I'm going." Checking that the roll of Christmas lights was still properly slung in place over her shoulder, Everly took a deep breath. If she didn't hurry, Annie would come check on her and the jig would be up. One look at her death grip on the ladder, and Annie Taggert would know Everly was afraid of heights.

Everly braved the first rung, then the second.

She had to do this. Besides being her best friend's grandma, Annie was also Everly's landlord. Everly earned her keep by helping out, an agreement brought on by necessity when Everly's mom sold the family house and moved to Ireland. Raking leaves, dusting, running errands, or climbing a ridiculously tall ladder to hang Christmas lights—the generous arrangement afforded her the opportunity to save for a down payment on a house. It was the single reason she kept her feet moving up the ladder.

Kenobi deserved *one* place to call his forever home.

Four rungs up. Then five. Everly paused to suck in another breath, not even realizing she'd been holding it. "Better send me pictures of that café soon," she muttered across the miles to her mom and climbed rungs six, seven, and eight.

If only waiting for Chloe had been an option, but her friend should be twenty miles or more down the road, headed to the Bangor airport to pick up a new rescue dog. Annie was convinced a storm was due to hit Snowy Falls in the next two days despite a weather forecast that argued the opposite. Her conviction didn't allow Everly to delay her most dreaded task.

"Now"—she gritted her teeth, taking rung number nine and the lowest one she could manage from if she went up on tiptoe—"or never," she added, edging up one more rung and pausing again.

Everly was fine as long as she didn't look down. Or the wind didn't wobble the ladder. But each time Kenobi barked, she automatically hugged the icy metal until she was convinced any threat was averted. Most of Kenobi's warnings turned out to be false alarms.

Annie was an angel to let the rambunctious lab stay at her house. Then again, Kenobi turned into a gentle lamb where Annie was concerned. Everly blamed it on the kitchen handouts—namely the endless supply of carrots she seemed to have.

"Kenobi, keep it down," she warned, keeping her eyes fixed on the eave of the roof.

A gust caught the ladder, lifting it an inch off the siding. She let out a squeak, riding the hard bounce back against the house with both eyes squeezed shut. She waited until the rocking stopped to let out a heavy breath and get back to work.

After plugging in the end of the strand to the previous one she'd already braved, Everly fished a few plastic clips from her pocket and hung the lights from the gutters until her arms couldn't reach. She swallowed, realizing her next task was to line the second-story window eave that jutted from the roof.

She'd have to *extend* the ladder.

"I can do this, right?" She squeezed her eyes shut, picturing Kenobi snuggled up with her on their own couch, watching the snow fall from the living room window. "Right."

With a deep breath, Everly lowered her foot. Kenobi let out a bark, startling her. Her foot slipped, then her gloved hands. She let out a tiny scream, tensing all her muscles and bracing for a distant, snowy landing.

The fall was shorter than expected. Much warmer too. Two strong arms enveloped her from behind, and Everly had to admit, it felt kind of nice to be held. A hint of peppermint danced in the air, along with a vaguely familiar woodsy scent she couldn't quite pin.

"What are you doing hanging Christmas lights in the *back* of the house?"

She stiffened at the sound of Noah Taggert's baritone voice. Four years had apparently *not* been long enough to erase it from her memory. Embarrassed and irritated, Everly shoved out of his arms and hopped away.

Kenobi raced up to her, effectively placing himself between them. Seemed the dog was apologizing for the accident he caused. Or taking credit, if his eager tail was any indication. Everly silently chided Chloe for neglecting to at least text her about Noah's holiday visit, until she remembered her best friend never knew about them to begin with. She rubbed a gloved hand over the dog's neck. "Guess you were trying to warn me, huh, boy?"

"What are you doing here?" Noah asked, less harsh this time.

"What does it look like I'm doing?" Everly pointed to the roof. "I'm hanging Christmas lights."

"No, I meant what are *you* doing *here*. At Grandma Annie's?"

It was a fair question. Annie was his grandma, not hers. But she didn't feel as if Noah deserved a full explanation. "Helping Annie."

"By putting lights on the *back* of the house where no one will see them?"

Everly folded both arms over her chest, the cold breeze biting now that she'd stopped moving and warm arms no longer held her. "Yes. That's what she wanted."

"Soup's ready," Grandma Annie hollered from the cracked kitchen window. "Hurry up before it gets cold."

One thing Everly learned living with Annie was that mealtimes were sacred. You didn't miss them without advance notice and detailed plans, and if you were late, everyone else suffered cold food while they waited.

"C'mon, Kenobi." Everly didn't wait to see whether Noah followed. With his whole family out of town, it was doubtful he had other lunch plans. *Too bad.* She could suffer one meal with the man who broke her heart. She swallowed the question she most longed to ask: *Why are you home, Noah?* She wasn't certain she'd care for the answer.

Inside, Everly shed her coat, annoyed that Noah had pilfered *her* hook. She hurried into the kitchen after Kenobi, ignoring Noah. Or at least she thought she was ignoring him. He still hadn't come through the door.

"It smells divine, Annie," Everly praised. Her stomach rumbled on cue, recalling the chicken tortilla soup described to her earlier that morning. She'd been looking forward to it ever since. "I'm starving!"

Everly grabbed the bowls, silverware, and napkins from the counter and set them around the table. Placing the last spoon, she felt Noah's presence in the doorway before he spoke.

"Which room did you want me to take?" he asked.

No. Oh, no. Noah couldn't be staying *here*. Not

when the entire Taggert house was empty. Common sense muffled her heart's protest. Of course he was staying here. The entire Taggert house *was* empty. Everly turned away, pointing Kenobi to his spot and buying herself a moment. *Well, dust bunnies.*

"One at the end of the hall ought to do," Annie said, completely unaffected by the arrangement. Of course, no one in the entire Taggert clan knew Everly and Noah had even started dating before he took off to help his uncle at Hope Valley Ranch. They agreed to wait to tell anyone until he came home. It was intended to be a Christmas surprise.

Only, he never came back, and she never knew why.

When Noah slipped away with his suitcase, Everly finally let out the breath she'd been holding. Kenobi, happy with the tortilla chip Annie snuck him, trotted to the table. In the short weeks they'd lived with Annie, he developed an easy mealtime routine that involved settling at Everly's feet and patiently waiting for handouts.

Though the pair had only been together two years, Everly couldn't remember life before her best friend found the rescued Labrador. Kenobi helped her feel less lonely with her mom now half a world away.

"How long did Noah say he was staying?" Everly asked Annie after glancing into the living room to make sure he wasn't back yet.

"Oh, through Christmas I imagine. Would be foolish of him to fly all this way and miss the family, wouldn't it?"

Disappointment struck Everly by surprise. It shouldn't matter that Noah wasn't home to stay. "Why *is* he back?"

"Grandma Annie, that soup smells even better than it did ten minutes ago," Noah said, rounding the corner while her words still hung in the air. He'd obviously overheard the question and had no interest in answering. It only made Everly more curious. He'd come alone, so it wasn't likely to introduce his family to a future—or current—wife.

Her eyes dropped automatically to his left hand. *Ringless.*

Everly looked away. She shouldn't care. Noah was the one who stopped calling and never came back.

"I hope you both brought big appetites. I made enough soup to feed the whole Taggert clan twice over, but you may be the only ones enjoying it. If they don't hurry and get back before that storm . . ." Her words drifted, gaze flicking to the wide picture window for just a moment. Grandma Annie had gone on and on about the big storm, due to hit Snowy Falls two days before Christmas, but the weatherman didn't seem to agree with her prediction. In fact, he forecasted clear skies, sunshine, and frigid temperatures.

"Maybe they'll stay in Cancun," Everly suggested. "It's certainly warmer there."

"Mom would never do that," Noah said with a laugh. "Not on purpose anyway."

"You're right, dear," Grandma Annie agreed, setting a bowl of tortilla chips on the table and finally settling into her seat. They bowed their heads for the blessing. Even Kenobi looked down at the floor, knowing better than to insist on handouts until they were finished.

As Everly ladled soup into bowls, Noah asked, "Grandma Annie, is there a reason you have Everly hanging lights in the *back* of the house?"

"You don't win lighting contests without going all out," Annie said matter-of-factly. "Plus, you know Peggy Ann can see right through those trees now that there's no leaves on them. I want her to know she has competition."

"I don't mind hanging them," Everly added, ignoring the raised eyebrow Noah gave her. He might remember her fear of heights. The one he learned about on their very first date while they were paused at the top of a Ferris wheel. "Keeps me busy since school's on break."

Noah raised an eyebrow, wordlessly calling her bluff.

Everly refused to acknowledge him, despite the stack of middle grade books on her nightstand waiting to be binge read over the break so she could decide if they belonged in her library. It was only one task of many she wanted to accomplish before school was back in session.

"Noah, why don't you give Everly a hand with the lights after lunch?"

Everly nearly choked on her spoonful of soup. A tortilla chip shot off the table courtesy of her elbow, launching itself right at Kenobi. He caught it midair. "I have it under control. I bet Noah's jet-lagged from flying."

"Oh, nonsense. You kids are young. Plus, I bet a little jet lag is nothing compared to long days working on that ranch. Probably a break, really."

Everly and Noah glanced at each other, both at a loss. "I don't mind helping," Noah finally said, flashing that kind smile that did her in when he'd asked her out on that first date. "I've got nothing but time on my hands until the family gets back."

"Oh, good!" Annie clapped her hands together, causing Kenobi to hop to his feet. "Everly has a whole list of Christmas chores. Maybe you can help. After the lights, we need to pick out a tree tonight."

Everly hid her panic with spoonfuls of soup. One day of shared Christmas chores wouldn't kill her, would it? With any luck, the Taggerts would be on a plane tonight and home by morning. Noah would be out of her hair as soon as they arrived.

But lately, Everly seemed to come up short where luck was concerned.

$\mathcal{N}$OAH

WHEN NOAH AGREED to help pick out a Christmas tree, he thought Grandma Annie was part of the equation. But she shooed Noah and Everly out the door, claiming she needed a nap. Even Kenobi got the boot. "I trust the two of you will find the perfect tree. And when you get back, you can decorate it."

"Look, it's easier if we just get this over with," Everly said after the door closed behind them. "I don't like it any more than you do, but it *is* Christmas."

The bitterness in her tone stung. Though he'd hoped to avoid running into Everly during his quick trip, it was only because he was convinced the sight of her happy—maybe even married—to another man would be too much to bear.

More surprising than finding her living with his grandma was that she was single. Chloe never mentioned it in any of her long-winded, gossip-filled emails. Considering she and Everly were best friends, Everly should've been part of the family recap. Whoever she'd been seeing years ago obviously hadn't lasted. Noah thought he'd been doing the honorable thing by bowing out, not forcing her to choose between them, but now he had to wonder.

He frowned as they backed out of the driveway. *What if I'd put up more of a fight back then? Would we be married now?* The silent questions circled in his mind and clenched at his heart as he drove through town and out on a small highway.

Kenobi stared out the passenger window, fogging it up with each breath through his nose, alert and excited at the slightest sign of movement. He let out a bark directed at a questionable snowman, which caused Noah and Everly to laugh, cracking apart the tension enough to make it bearable.

He'd always pictured her with a dog, and was happy she found one. One of Chloe's rescues, no doubt.

"Did you really come home to surprise your family for Christmas?" Everly asked as the last few clusters of houses thinned.

He loved Maine for its scenery, especially in

winter. The heavy snow resting in tall trees and the way it glistened in the sunlight. Houses nestled among the tree-covered hills, all with that old New England feel. Noah drank it in, buying himself time before he answered. "No."

"Didn't think so."

It was foolish to want Everly to ask him why, but he felt the yearning just the same. When she didn't press, he let it go. A couple of days from now, it wouldn't matter anyway.

Noah assumed that Johnson's Tree Farm was still in business, and Everly didn't correct him when he turned off the highway and onto the dirt road that led there. His family had picked out their tree there every year until Mom decided a fake one was safer with a thirsty dog in the house. Considering they were all in Cancun right now, that fake tree was probably a wise switch, even with Pongo likely staying with a neighbor.

"How long have you been living with Grandma Annie?" he asked.

"Since October."

"Mind if I ask why?"

"Yeah, I do mind. Noah, slow down. You'll miss the last turn."

He eased his foot off the gas and onto the brake, taking the turn with a little more speed than he intended. But he didn't allow the surprise to show in his expression. During the first hard weeks on the ranch, he fantasized about life with Everly at Christmas. He imagined them coming to this tree farm, walking hand in hand through the rows until her face lit up at the sight of the perfect one.

Noah loved Christmas. At least, he used to.

Lately, it didn't hold the same special meaning. Though they celebrated the holiday on the ranch, it was mostly with a hearty spread. Food and conversation won over decorations and presents. The animals still needed feeding and tending. They didn't care much that it was a holiday. Noah spent last Christmas treating a mare with a broken leg.

Noah followed Everly and Kenobi up the long, wooden-plank walk to the store, unable to keep his gaze from sweeping over her. In that red coat with its fur-lined hood and fuzzy earmuffs, he couldn't help but find her adorable. The urge to drape his arm over her shoulders and pull her tight against him was unsettling, so he shook it away.

"You coming?" she asked, holding the door.

Noah nodded and followed her in. The fragrance of cinnamon-scented pinecones hit him immediately and he glanced around for the cause. Sure enough, a crate of them sat near the door with a big sale sign. "Did Grandma Annie mention what kind of tree she wanted us to get?" he asked.

"How should I know? She's your grandma." Instead of the snippiness from earlier, a twinkle— however brief—danced in Everly's eyes. "She said she trusted our judgment. There's enough ornaments, lights, and garland to cover three trees. I'm betting that bigger is better."

"A big, fat tree it is."

Once they picked up a tree tag from the counter and Kenobi received a treat, they slipped out the back into the gated selection of Christmas trees. Light snowflakes dusted the air, but the chilly wind that'd stuck with them through hanging up the last of the lights calmed for their stroll.

"Hard to believe there's a big snowstorm headed this way, isn't it?" Everly said, stopping to assess a thick, stumpy tree then moving on.

"I checked the forecast. I didn't see anything beyond an inch of snow headed this way before Christmas." Grandma Annie loved her weather. But more than that, she loved proving the weatherman wrong. She was right about fifty percent of the time, or so Noah recalled. But he doubted her blizzard prediction would hold true this time. He had to believe it wouldn't so his family could make it home and he could fly back to Montana before he did something foolish. Like fall in love with Everly all over again.

"Hope you're right, or your family might not make it back until after Christmas."

Noah stiffened at the thought he'd been trying to push away. It wasn't just the antsy feeling of being in his hometown and around Everly. He was needed

—*expected*—at the ranch. The vet from the Wilson ranch down the road was covering in his absence, but it felt unfair to expect her to do that through the holiday.

Kenobi let out a bark, plopping his rear down in the snow. "I think he found our tree," Noah said.

"*That* tree? The scraggly, thin one?" Everly shook her head with a laugh. Even after all this time, her smile still made his heart pitter-patter. "I'm not a Taggert, but I know your family well enough to say that tree would never pass. Grandma Annie would send us right back to return it and you know it. C'mon, Kenobi. Better luck next time."

They slowly wandered the rows of trees, neither in a particular hurry to get back to Grandma Annie's and be put to work. But the traveling was starting to catch up with Noah, and a yawn escaped.

"How long are you staying?" Everly asked.

The truth sounded so harsh in his head. "Not sure," he answered, evading. "Depends on the rest of the family, I guess."

"You're not moving home, then?"

Despite his best efforts, Noah failed to dissect what really lingered in that question. "No."

"That ranch has really grown on you, then. Why did—"

Noah's phone made a rare chime, announcing a call. He scooped it out of his coat pocket curious if it was family or the ranch. He'd left Reed, the head foreman, a message to call him back. "Sorry, got to take this. I'll catch up with you."

He pretended not to notice the way her smile faded into a frown and instead turned in the opposite direction to answer the call. "Reed, can you hear me?"

"In town, so you're crystal clear today." Since Arthur's death, Reed had taken over running operations at the ranch. If Noah decided to keep the family property, he'd still have Reed manage it. The man had a knack for the whole operation. Noah was happy simply to do his part tending to the health of the animals and pitching in when they needed extra help with chores. "Did you make it to Maine?"

"Yeah." He turned, scanning for Everly. He didn't see her but spotted the flash of yellow a few rows over.

"How's the family?"

"Gone."

"Gone?"

"Everyone but Grandma Annie." Noah gave Reed the short version about his sister's impulsive decision that sent everyone on a retrieval mission. "With any luck they'll be back in a day or two, but—"

"You'll be gone longer than you planned." Reed's tone betrayed no emotion, only objectivity that no doubt meant he was figuring out how to adjust. "Do what you have to do, Noah. We have things covered here."

If Uncle Arthur's will hadn't been so specific about the time of year he wanted his ashes scattered, Noah'd board a plane tonight and return in the spring. The only reason he'd waited this long to come home was because of that stipulation regarding the week of Christmas. "I'm sorry—"

"Don't be. You haven't been home for years. It's Christmas. Why don't you stay? Enjoy the holiday with your family when they get back."

"Right."

"Shoot me an email when you make it to the airport," Reed added. "And eat a few slices of that legendary pumpkin pie for me, the one you're always going on about during the holidays."

"That I *can* do," Noah added with a laugh before he ended the call. Despite the conversation, guilt still seeped in at the extra work his absence would cause. Noah dropped the phone back in his coat pocket and searched for Everly.

He found her stopped at an intersection, scanning her options before picking a direction. "Was that your family?" she asked.

"No. The ranch. Had to let them know I'm delayed."

He waited for her to ask why he never came back. Or to ask anything else about his life in Montana. Instead, she asked, "You really didn't know your family went after your sister?"

Noah shoved his cold hands in his pockets and

kicked at the fresh powder as they strolled down a promising aisle of fat, lush trees. "Chloe usually keeps me up to speed on the family, but I didn't get an email from her this week. My cell . . ." He let the sentence trail off. Everly no doubt remembered his cell reception was practically nonexistent on the ranch. He only kept one so he could check messages and make the occasional call while in town.

In their haste to save Blakely, no one thought to leave him a voicemail. Of course, had anyone suspected Noah might show up this year, they might have. It was his own fault for choosing such an isolated life.

He slowed as his gaze landed on a plump, tall tree and pointed. "What about that one over there?"

Kenobi trotted happily through the snow in front of them, stopping on his way to Noah's choice to stick his nose through the branches of another.

"You're right." When they reached it, Everly flashed him a smile, but it didn't reach her eyes. "This is the perfect tree."

He wanted to know everything that had happened in her life while he was gone. Well, everything except who she'd dated. Noah could live without knowing that. He cleared his throat, focusing on this one, perfect moment.

"What do you think, Kenobi?" she asked, only reminding him how easy it'd been to fall for her the first time.

At his name, the dog jerked his head toward Everly and barked.

For reasons Noah didn't care to explore, he wasn't ready to return to Grandma Annie's. He rather liked spending time with Everly now that the hostility had slipped away. He feared returning to the house would shatter the dusting of magic.

Noah draped the tag on a branch. "Guess we got our tree."

CHAPTER 4

$\mathscr{E}$VERLY

"Kenobi, huh?" Sitting at the stop sign leading back onto the highway, Noah glanced at Everly, causing her pulse to double, butterflies fluttering. She shouldn't be this affected anymore by those deep brown eyes. Especially since *he* was the one who didn't come home.

"Yeah, he seems to like the name," she answered, scratching the lab between the ears in an effort to divert her focus. He'd lodged his head between the two bucket seats after hearing his name, eyes alert on the road ahead.

"I thought you hated *Star Wars*."

"I don't *hate* it."

"Didn't think you loved it enough to name your dog—"

"That was his name when I got him."

"And you didn't change it?" The twinkle in Noah's eyes, warning her that he was teasing, forced Everly to look away. Sleep. She needed a good night's sleep. Tomorrow she'd be better able to handle her reactions. Tomorrow he wouldn't catch her off guard.

"I tried. Believe me."

"Was he one of Chloe's rescues?" Noah asked, thick woods giving way to rows of houses.

She should feel relief to be within the city limits, but the sooner they returned to Annie's, the sooner they'd be forced to work together. Instead of decorating the tree, Everly yearned for a warm blanket, a cup of Annie's famous cocoa, and one of the many books stacked haphazardly on her nightstand. *Will this day never end?*

"Chloe called me the day she picked him up. Thought he'd be perfect for me." Everly swallowed when Noah turned down a residential street instead of following the main road through downtown as she'd hoped. It didn't matter that a good, deserving family had purchased her childhood home. It was still hard to drive by the Victorian with someone else living there. "Got Kenobi two years ago," she continued, mostly to distract herself. "His last owner surrendered him when he moved to the West Coast. I guess he wasn't the only owner, either."

Kenobi gave her a lick on the cheek before focusing his attention out the back window again. Two kids worked together, lifting the head of a snowman into place under Kenobi's laser-focused stare. The lab barely breathed until the crest of hill made them disappear.

"You two seem to make a good pair," Noah said.

"He's wonderful," she added, thankful today, like every day, that he found his way into her life. "A handful, but wonderful."

At another stop sign, Noah turned his full attention on her. "Did we just make it three whole minutes without a single jab?"

Everly rolled her eyes, but her smile was impossible to contain. A hint of one slipped out despite her best efforts. "I'd say don't get used to it, but you won't be around long enough for that to happen anyway."

"And *there* goes our streak."

Everly let out a strained laugh. Dozens of questions zipped through her mind when it came to Noah Taggert, but the loudest one demanded to know why he never came home. Part of her had always suspected—feared—that he found someone else. She formed the question in her head, rearranging and editing the words. Before she could give it voice, Noah spoke.

"How's your mom doing?" he asked, nodding to

the two-story Victorian with a wraparound porch she used to call home.

"Fine, last I heard." The closer they came to it, the more impossible it was to evade the topic. Not quite a trade secret, Everly still wasn't keen to discuss everything with the man who'd broken his promise to her. How could she put into words that her mom and aunt leaving the country had been the last straw on a tall pile that started with him?

"You two aren't fight—" Noah stopped his question as he slowed the truck past the corner house. "Wait, who's living here? Did your mom *sell* it?"

Everly squirmed in her seat, eager for the house to fade in the rearview mirror. "Yes."

"But why—"

Kenobi let out a series of barks, turning his attention across the street and toward the house he'd called home for almost two years. The poor dog had been through so many homes. It was one of her biggest motivators for buying a place of her own. Their own. She wanted Kenobi to have one consistent home he'd never have to leave.

"Please. Keep driving," Everly pleaded in a soft voice.

His hand flinched toward the console, as if he meant to take her hand, but he fiddled with a heater vent instead. "I don't understand."

Moisture dotted the corners of her eyes, but she

couldn't pinpoint the emotion threatening the tears. "Please?"

Without further interrogation, Noah obliged. He waited until the last turn to Annie's to break the silence. He lightly patted her gloved hand, like any friend might. "Please tell me your mom is okay? Did something happen to her—"

"Mom's alive and well." She pulled her hand free, remembering all too well the powerful effects his touch had on her. Regaining her composure, she added, "And living quite happily in *Ireland*."

Noah's sigh of relief was so extreme that Everly felt compelled to apologize for the scare. But before she could utter the words, the flicker of headlights drew her attention toward Annie's. "Does your sister know you're home?" Everly asked when she recognized the silhouette of Chloe's rescue van pulling alongside the curb.

"No."

"Well, she's about to." Everly hopped out of the truck half a second after Noah shifted into park. Clipping the leash on Kenobi, she waited for him to leap out of the back seat and closed the door behind him.

"Everly, did you get a new truck?" Chloe called over her shoulder, fiddling with something in the passenger seat. "I thought you were saving—"

"It's Noah's truck," Everly cut in. The less Noah

knew about her life and her goals, the better. If he didn't know, he couldn't pretend to care. Her heart was safer this way.

"Noah?"

"Surprise," Noah called to Chloe.

Everly watched from the driveway as her best friend's face morphed from confusion, to shock, to elation. Whatever she'd been tinkering with in the passenger seat was forgotten the moment recognition flashed in her bright eyes. She bolted toward Noah, tackling him in a hug and taking them both down into a snowbank.

Kenobi barked and pulled against the leash, no doubt yearning to join in the fun.

"You didn't tell me you were coming home!" Chloe smacked Noah—still laid out in the snow—with her red mitten. She shuffled to her feet, extending a hand.

"In all fairness," Everly heard Noah say as the two dusted snow from their coats, "you didn't tell me the whole family took off to Mexico."

Chloe returned to her van, reaching inside for a tote bag and slinging it over her shoulder. "Yes, I did."

"When?" Noah dug in his pocket for his phone.

"I sent you an email today."

He draped an arm around Chloe and gave her a side hug as they made their way up the driveway. "A lot of good that did me."

Chloe stopped short of the stairs leading toward the front door, her curious gaze bouncing between the two of them as she scratched an eager Kenobi between the ears. "Wait. What were the *two* of you doing in your truck?"

"Grandma Annie sent us to pick out a Christmas tree." Everly pointed to the bed of the truck and the tips of the evergreen peeking over the top. "I thought you were on a rescue run to Bangor," she said, changing the topic and feeling guiltier than she should for not alerting Chloe that her brother had showed up unannounced. *Good grief. I really am exhausted.*

"Flight got delayed, so Belle won't be here until tomorrow. Heading out first thing in the morning. Since I'm still in town, Grandma Annie insisted I take her to Reindeer Bingo tonight. She's determined to win the jackpot this year. With everyone else gone —well, I *thought* everyone else was gone—I didn't want to say no."

"Reindeer Bingo?" Noah repeated, eyebrows drawn in. "Is that a real thing?"

"Of course it is." Chloe gently shoved at Everly, encouraging her to climb the stairs and get inside. "You'd know that if you came home more than once every four years."

With a shake of his head, Noah said, "I'll be right in. Need to grab the tree."

Inside, Everly took her time unbuttoning her

coat and carefully placing her boots beneath the bench. If Chloe was taking Annie to bingo tonight, that would leave her alone with Noah to decorate the tree. Panic caused her pulse to double again, all because of Noah Taggert. This had to stop. What existed between them before was no more. If only she could get her heart to receive that message.

"Grandma Annie, I'm here." Chloe slid the tote bag filled with wrapped gifts from her shoulder and set it on the living room floor. "You'll put those under the tree once it's up?" she asked Everly in a low voice. "Brought them in case there's any truth to this snowstorm business."

"I'll take care of them," Everly promised.

"I'm coming," Annie called from the kitchen, the clicking of claws giving away Kenobi's new location. Everly found him sitting obediently at the edge of the kitchen island, focused on a piece of carrot Annie dangled.

"That dog really loves his veggies, huh?" Chloe asked with a laugh as she and Everly stood in the kitchen.

"He's a carrot addict. Your grandma spoils him."

"It's not spoiling, dear." A twinkle danced in Annie's eyes. "It's what motivates him. Healthier than donuts and cheaper than steak, right?" Annie tossed the carrot in the air and Kenobi caught it with ease, crunching it happily between his chompers. "Did you find a tree?"

"Yes," Everly answered. "Noah's bringing it inside now."

"A big, fat one I hope?" Chloe chimed in.

"It's no Charlie Brown tree, that's for sure," Noah said from behind, startling a quiet squeak from Everly. For a man who lived in cowboy boots, he shouldn't have the ability to sneak up on her. Everly blamed Annie's shoes-off-in-the-house rule.

"Let's get it in some water so we can get going," Annie said. "I want to get good seats right up front."

"We?" Everly and Noah asked in unison.

"You don't want to miss Reindeer Bingo. Jackpot's a thousand dollars!"

Everly felt relieved she hadn't been sipping on some of that hot cocoa she craved. She might've choked on it. She'd spotted fliers around town for the holiday bingo festivities all week, but she apparently missed the detail about the enormous jackpot. In the overall scheme of things, a thousand dollars wouldn't bump her nest egg up enough for a house down payment. But it'd move her timeline up by at least a month.

Noah let out a yawn, but whether real or fake was up for debate. "I might stay here," he said. "I'm pretty wiped."

Everly felt both relieved and disappointed, which made no sense. She needed space from Noah and this was the perfect excuse. Tomorrow they'd be forced to work together decorating the tree and doing whatever holiday chores Annie came up with. She should be thrilled to avoid him for the remainder of the evening.

"Nonsense." Annie sent him a dismissive wave. "This won't go too late, and they'll have loads of cookies."

Noah scrubbed a hand over his face. Arguing with Annie was futile. They all knew it. "Will there be coffee?"

"Enough to fuel that entire ranch of yours three times over. Any more questions?"

Everly and Chloe glanced at each other, fighting back a giggle.

"What about Kenobi?" Noah asked, filling the can Annie set aside with water. "Can he be trusted not to drink the tree dry?"

"He'll come along, of course."

"Really?" Everly had never been to Reindeer Bingo, but she was surprised it was a dog-friendly event.

"Why not? I already packed him a baggie full of carrots. He'll be on his best behavior, won't you?" Annie smiled at the dog with such rapture Everly almost hated the thought of eventually moving out and separating the two.

Chloe looped one arm through Everly's and the other through Noah's and ushered them toward the door. "We better get going so we can get those prime seats."

"That's the spirit!" Annie said cheerfully behind them. "Let's go win us a jackpot!"

CHAPTER 5

NOAH

THE LAST TIME Noah stepped foot in the Snowy Falls Community Center was when his entire family packed around a table in support of the local Legion and their annual turkey supper. It was the last gathering they had as a family before Noah boarded a plane destined for Billings.

Now the same hall was decorated in green and silver garland. Dozens of colored reindeer pictures, courtesy of the local elementary school, covered the walls. Red tablecloths with various holiday-themed centerpieces filled the room. The light chatter of conversation mingled with jazzy Christmas music.

Noah paused behind the ladies to savor the moment. It felt like home.

"Load us up," Grandma Annie said to the woman taking money at the door. "We want to play for the jackpot."

Kenobi paced short circles around Everly, eager to explore his new environment. If they hadn't all ridden together in one vehicle, Noah might've had an excuse to leave early. But he was far too exhausted to trek all the way across town, up some of the steepest hills, for an extra hour or two of sleep.

"We'll find a table," Chloe said, latching onto his arm and dragging him along. The Taggert women were some of the most stubborn he'd ever met, and Noah knew better than to fight it when one of them set their mind to something. So he followed, leaving Everly to handle Kenobi and Grandma to figure out the rest.

Noah scanned the room for a coffee station and found two in opposite corners. His yawns, unlike earlier, were now genuine. "How did we get roped into this?" he asked when Chloe pointed at a table.

"You showed up one day too late to hop on a plane to Cancun with the rest of them."

"Heard anything about that?" he asked, hoping his family was at the airport right now, waiting to board a late flight headed for Maine. The sooner they returned, the sooner he could fulfill Uncle Arthur's final wish and get back to Hope Valley.

Chloe shimmied out of her coat, draping it on the back of her chair. Her already curly blonde hair expanded the moment she removed her hat to shove it in the hood of her coat. "No, nothing yet. But we told them not to call until they had news. The priority was to stop the wedding and talk Blakely off the ledge."

"What was she thinking anyway?"

"You're really asking me that?"

Their youngest sister was also their most impulsive sibling. Though Blakely had pulled a few stunts throughout the years, running off to elope was by far the most serious. "This lawyer she's trying to marry any good?"

"No. Not only does he *not* like dogs, but Grimm met him once," Chloe said, referring to their brother Will's Great Dane. "Tried to bite his hand off."

"Sweet Grimm?"

"That's the one."

"Perfect table," Grandma Annie said in approval, dropping a stack of bingo cards and a few daubers onto the table. "Near the caller *and* the cookies." She shed her coat in the seat next to Noah's, snuck Kenobi a carrot, then took off for her own snacks.

"Still surprised they allow dogs," Noah said, looking around and noticing Kenobi was the only four-legged member in attendance.

"They don't," Chloe answered. "But would *you* tell our grandma no?"

Noah laughed. "Point taken." Two steps on his way to acquire the strongest dose of caffeine he could find, he stopped. "Anyone else want coffee?"

"Not me," Chloe said. "I need to sleep tonight. This Belle I'm picking up tomorrow has been promised to keep me on my toes. I'm told she's an escape artist with the energy of a squirrel on a caffeine IV."

"Everly?" he asked, remembering she liked a scoop of sugar and caramel creamer.

"Sure."

He took his time with the coffee, filling the dinky Styrofoam cups and procuring all the extras. With cups this small, he'd be up between each round of bingo for refills. The stack of bingo cards promised several rounds. When he returned to the table, he was surprised to find half of the seats already occupied.

"You all remember my grandson, Noah?" Grandma Annie said to an elderly couple as he set down the cups.

With the grogginess he hoped coffee would cure, it took Noah several seconds to place them. "Mr. and Mrs. Hartman," Noah said, extending his hand in greeting. "Good to see you."

"You still working out at that ranch in Montana?" Harold, a local woodworker, was also related to Noah's former boss. The squint in the old man's eyes implied he was willing to hold a grudge for his brother Jim.

"Yes, sir. Hope Valley Ranch." When Noah called to let Jim Hartman know he wouldn't be returning to the Hartman Horse Farm four years ago, the news hadn't been well received. On instinct, Noah scanned the room in search of Jim and his wife Nancy, momentarily relieved not to spot them.

"We're sorry to hear about your uncle," Harold's wife Maisey said as Noah slid into his chair.

"Thank you."

"I hoped Arthur would come back for a visit," Maisey added. "We always enjoyed his company. Shame he didn't."

"Ranch kept him quite busy. Keeps us *all* busy." Noah flashed a smile as he doctored his coffee, doing his best to avert his eyes from Everly sitting across from him. Still, he caught the fleeting flash of gratitude when she noticed her creamer packets. "Arthur always intended to come back to see everyone." It was his one regret before passing, and the reason he asked Noah to take some of his ashes back to Snowy Falls.

"You moving home, then?" Harold asked.

Noah felt several sets of eyes land on him and swallowed hard. He bought himself a few seconds with a piping-hot sip of coffee. "No, I'm just back for a few days. I'm the vet out there now." It didn't seem important to mention the ranch was willed to go to him a year after Arthur's passing, so he didn't. "Hard enough to steal a few days away as it is."

"Too bad. I'm sure your folks miss having you around," Maisey said, patting his hand. "Annie, you heard anything yet about Blakely?"

"Not yet. Robyn promised to call in the morning with an update."

"I still can't believe she took off like that."

Noah sipped his coffee, grateful for the momentary reprieve as he allowed his attention to drift away from the conversation about his sister. *Nothing new to learn there*. Instead, his mind spun with his own thoughts. He wasn't sure what he'd do in Snowy Falls if he did decide to move home. Despite the profuse apologies, his former boss had been put out that he'd saved Noah's position for him. Jim was known to hold a grudge. Even *if* Noah wanted to return, he doubted his former job would ever be available to him.

Sure, Maine had its fill of horse farms. But he didn't hold out high hopes that any of them were looking to hire a full-time vet. Nor would any of those positions grant Noah the freedom he had at Hope Valley.

But Everly is here.

Grandma Annie slid a tablet of bingo sheets in front of him, saving him from his pointless thoughts.

Better yet, it gave him an excuse to avoid Everly's curious gaze from across the table. Though their dating history was brief, she'd learned to read him like a book and always knew when something was troubling his mind.

"They'll explain it all in a few minutes," Grandma Annie told him, pushing a dauber into his hand, "but we're going to play a few rounds. They'll go quick. Get that dauber at the ready and pay attention."

Noah fought another yawn. "A few rounds?"

"Winners get special tokens for the final game. Some pretty darn good advantages in those tokens." She handed him a bingo card filled with different reindeer and numbers. "This card is for the big one. I don't want you to get your hopes up since I'm planning to take the jackpot home this year. But it'll be fun just the same."

Noah draped his arm around Grandma Annie and squeezed her in a side hug. "I've missed you."

"Missed you too, Noah." She planted a kiss on his cheek that no doubt left behind a faint lipstick print. He didn't dare wipe it off. "You should come home more. Better yet, *move* home. Doesn't feel right to have you so far away."

His flickering gaze caught Everly's, the temptation to do as everyone suggested stronger than ever. Could he win a second chance with Everly if he did? He shook away the thought, blaming the jet lag.

"Stock up on your cookies and coffee, folks. We're about to get started," the bingo caller announced, giving him an excuse to look away. Fantasies aside, moving home wasn't an option. If he forfeited the ranch— He shook away the thought. He couldn't let that happen.

CHAPTER 6

*E*VERLY

Everly woke to a cold, wet nose pressed against her cheek. Large brown eyes stared at her. She squeezed her own shut and pretended to sleep again. Kenobi licked her on the cheek. She couldn't stop the laugh. "Okay, okay. I'm up."

She rubbed the spot between his ears that made him moan with delight, feeling grateful yet again for this wonderful dog who loved to snuggle and sleep on the bed throughout the night. It made her feel safe and brought comfort, despite the occasional paw to the back in the middle of the night.

Over his furry head and stack of books, she noticed the clock.

"We have to scoot!" She tossed back the covers, urging Kenobi off the bed. With only two minutes until her mom was due to Skype, Everly didn't want to risk missing the call. She slipped on a hoodie, a pair of fuzzy socks, and left her messy hair in its lazy bun at the top of her head.

Laptop tucked under the crook of her arm, the aroma of freshly baked cinnamon rolls teased her as she slipped down a hallway to the corner office where the strongest Wi-Fi signal lived. Breakfast would have to wait, which her grumbling stomach didn't much care for. But at least Everly could avoid Noah for a little while longer.

Last night at bingo, everyone kept asking him if he was planning to move back home now that his uncle was gone. Something unspoken danced in his eyes each time, though she could hardly guess what. His answer was always the same—*no*—yet she felt something in him giving. Everly knew better than to get her hopes up, but it was happening just the same.

He's not staying.

Five seconds after logging in to her account, the call came through the computer screen.

"Hey, Mom!" She gave a little wave as Kenobi pushed his way into her lap and lifted his head toward the screen. Everly pointed at the camera to guide his attention, but his nose pressed against it, blocking out the screen.

"There's my granddog!"

Kenobi's head tilted at the voice he recognized.

"She's right there." Everly pointed at the screen, urging Kenobi back from the screen to display more than his nose. The playful confusion went on for a few minutes before Kenobi's attention was stolen by something outside. Everly suspected a bird.

"How are you, dear? Enjoying your break?" Mom asked, tucking loose, silvering strands behind her ears. She looked a little tired, if the slight bags under her eyes said anything, but her sparkling eyes and smile were genuine. Everly was happy her mom and Aunt Suz were pursuing a lifelong dream together.

"What break?" Everly teased, remembering that her mom didn't know about the Taggert family drama.

"I know you better than that. I'm sure you're antsy as ever to get into that library of yours and get to work. I still think it's bad luck to take down the Christmas decorations until *after* the holiday."

"You'll be happy to hear that I haven't been to the library once this week." Everly was waiting on a shipment of approved books due to arrive any day. Even Annie wouldn't deny her the pleasure of slipping away for a few hours to catalogue them and give them new homes when they showed up.

"Are you feeling okay, honey? Not coming down with a cold, are you?"

Everly laughed, rolling her eyes on purpose. "No, Mom. I'm also helping Annie get ready for the Taggert family Christmas because the whole lot of them are in Cancun." *Except Chloe and Noah.*

"Cancun?"

Everly launched into the story about Blakely, conveniently leaving out the detail about Noah showing up unexpectedly. The fewer questions about him, the better. "She's convinced a blizzard's on its way, so if they don't get on a plane soon, they might not make it back."

"I hope they do, but I can think of worse things than spending Christmas on a beach."

"How's business?" Her lab punctuated Everly's question with a few barks out the window. "Kenobi, *shh!*"

"Booming since the grand opening!" Mom's smile eased away the sting of her absence. She and Aunt Suz moved to Ireland three months ago to follow a lifelong dream of opening a café there. The abrupt announcement of the move and selling the house left Everly in a pinch to find a new place to live. The arrangement with Annie was an unexpected blessing.

"That's great news, Mom."

"They especially love our holiday concoctions. I hope you can visit soon. You'd love this quaint little town. I miss you, sweetie, and I'm so sorry we can't spend Christmas together this year. But I really do love it here. Your aunt Suz does, too. If you ever get tired of that library . . ."

"You know I won't, but thanks for the offer."

Kenobi barked again, drawing Everly's attention to the window. Fresh powder covered the driveway, except for the strips Noah had already shoveled. He *would* have the nerve to go outside in a fitted T-shirt and no coat. Even from up here, Everly couldn't help but notice how his biceps flexed with each scoop. *Stupid muscles*. She'd bet her next paycheck he did far more on that ranch than tend to sick animals.

"Earth to Everly," Mom called.

"Sorry." She tore her gaze from the window, turning her chair slightly to avoid further accidental glances. Telling Mom that Noah was staying with Annie wouldn't do any good. Mom had always liked Noah and had high hopes for the two of them, until he decided not to come home, and broke her heart. Mom's opinion wasn't so high anymore.

A knock at the door preceded the aroma of the cinnamon roll Annie held. "Sorry to interrupt."

"Hi, Annie," Mom said with a wave.

"Hi, Maureen. How's Ireland?"

"Lovely as ever. Is that a homemade cinnamon roll? I can practically smell it through the screen."

Annie set the plate on the desk next to the laptop. "They're Noah's favorite. Thought I'd whip up a batch for him since I put him to work so early."

"Noah?"

"He came back for a surprise visit," Everly said with a shoulder shrug, hoping she sounded indifferent enough for her mom to believe it. "Wasn't that nice of him?" The last was a warning, reminding Mom that none of the Taggerts knew about her history with Noah. She met her mom's gaze over thousands of miles and an invisible Internet connection. *Please. Don't say it.*

"How nice." Mom's smile could fool the best of them, including Annie it seemed. But Everly wasn't deceived. Mom had been there to pick up the pieces after Everly finally accepted that Noah wasn't coming home.

"Did Everly tell you I took home the bingo jackpot last night?" Annie asked, slipping Kenobi a carrot. It was the only thing that could entice him more than the goodie on Everly's plate.

"The jackpot?"

"A thousand big ones. Won it just like I told these kids I would. Maybe *now* they'll believe me about the snowstorm." Everly allowed the two women to chat, trying and failing to ignore Noah through the window as she ate her cinnamon roll. He made quick work of the driveway and moved on to the sidewalks. With any luck, Grandma Annie would keep him too preoccupied with chores to help with the tree later.

"Well, I'll let you two get back to your chat," Annie said. "Didn't mean to crash the conversation."

"Never," Mom said. "Thanks again, Annie, for looking after my daughter. I know she can handle herself, but it does make me feel better knowing she won't be spending Christmas alone."

Annie patted Everly on the shoulder. "We'd never let her do that, even if we had to kidnap her."

Everly stayed silent until Annie, taking Kenobi with her, closed the door. But she wasn't quick enough with her own words to divert the inevitable topic of conversation now that Mom knew about Noah.

"Noah Taggert is staying in the *same* house? Sweetie, I wasn't planning to be stateside for a while, but this might be an exception. Are you sure you're okay? I can hop on the next flight—"

"Mom. I'm fine. Put down the bear claws. He's only here for a day or two until his family gets back. He's more than eager to get back on a plane to Montana."

"Still, keep your distance. That boy is quicksand."

"I wish I could hug you right now." Thankfully, the conversation shifted from Noah to the last few days at school before the break. Everly loved talking about the kids and their love of books. "I made sure no one went home without at least one book this break. Most took two." She went on to explain how she'd carefully selected books for her many students and was already elbow-deep in a new stack of books she could recommend in January.

"You really do love that job, don't you?"

"With all my heart." Despite how much Everly enjoyed the break, she did miss the bustle of students.

"Looks like my lunch break is over, sweetie. Can't leave Aunt Suz in there all by her lonesome a minute longer or I'll hear about it for sure." With cheerful goodbyes, they arranged for a Christmas Day call outside the normal weekly one.

Call ended, Everly carried her empty plate to the kitchen, hoping to sneak another cinnamon roll even if it spoiled her lunch. If she didn't find a house of her own soon, she'd need to get a gym membership to counter the effects of Annie's amazing cooking.

"Stealing *my* cinnamon rolls?" Noah's deep voice startled a squeak out of her. Seemed he was doing that a lot lately. Everly spun away from the pan, but the gooey frosting coated two of her fingers.

In those Wranglers and the fitted black T-shirt, Noah looked every bit as handsome as the first day she discovered she had a crush on him. It wasn't fair when she looked like she just rolled out of bed— mostly because she had—with her brown hair twisted in a messy knot at the top of her head.

Despite her disheveled appearance, Everly stood her ground. "What makes them yours?"

"I shoveled the driveway. They're my reward."

Everly looked back at the pan. "You need *all* of those?"

"I earned *all* of those."

Everly raised a playful eyebrow at Noah.

"What are you doing?" he asked.

She flashed him a smirk half a second before she spun around and jabbed her finger right through the middle of the same roll she'd tried to pilfer before he caught her. "That one is mine. I *earned* it."

Noah stood close now, amused it seemed by their little game. If she had any sense, she'd end the antics now. "How?"

"I hung Christmas lights."

"*I* helped you."

"I hung plenty before you got here." Everly reached for the roll, but Noah caught her arm. She searched for something clever to say, but words failed her. Her gaze kept landing on his lips, no matter how many times she looked away from them. She still remembered the way her entire body ignited with life at his kiss.

"If we're keeping score—"

Kenobi's barks preceded his claws scrabbling with speed against the tile floor. He charged right for them, bumping hard into Noah's legs. He fell against Everly, catching her with his arm an inch before they both knocked elbows into the pan of rolls.

"Kenobi!" Everly scolded. "You're not supposed to be in the kitchen."

"Thought I heard some commotion," Annie said, causing Everly to hop a step back and abandon her cinnamon roll mission for coffee instead. "Noah, let me get you a plate."

Noah flashed her a victorious smile when Annie wasn't looking. Everly narrowed her eyes in response. When he scooped up *her* roll on his plate, she narrowed them even more.

"Can you two help get that tree up and decorated today? I think we'll need new lights. Some of the strands are quite old. You can charge them to my account down at the store."

"Of course," answered Everly, watching with longing as Noah carried her cinnamon roll to the table and ate it with torturous leisure.

"Grandma Annie, these are *amazing*," said Noah, wriggling his eyebrows at Everly.

Everly turned her back to him. "Anything else you need done today?"

"The tree's the priority," Annie said. "Cookies if there's time, but those can wait until tomorrow as long as we get them done earlier in the day. Power might go out by nightfall, so be prepared."

"Grandma Annie, the forecast doesn't show another snowflake until the day after Christmas,"

Noah countered. "The couple inches from last night are it. What's this storm prediction all about?"

Annie clapped her hand on Noah's shoulder. "When you get to be my age, you learn to judge these things by experience. I'd wager my jackpot winnings on this storm coming. I'm not going to make the bet because I promised the birthday club I'd buy lunch today if I won, but if I did, believe I'd double my money."

Suspecting Annie was soon headed out the door, Everly inched her way closer to the pan of cinnamon rolls. Since Noah stole hers, she'd have to choose another.

"Oh, Noah, your mom called this morning," Annie added.

Everly perked at the news. Hopeful the Taggerts would make it back for the holidays. The sooner this house was filled with people, the better. Most of them would bombard Noah with attention, and the others would keep Everly a safe distance away.

"And?" Noah asked between bites.

"They've booked their return tickets. God willing, their flight leaves tonight, but they're still trying to put the kibosh on her plans. She's not married. *Yet.*" Annie shook her head and added in a mutter, "Your brother should've brought Grimm. Maybe the dog would get through to her."

"You leaving?" Noah asked.

"Got to finish up my Christmas shopping, then

lunch. I trust you two can handle the tree without my supervision? Leftover soup in the fridge."

Everly dished up her second roll without regret. She'd need it to survive another day left alone with Noah Taggert.

CHAPTER 7

$\mathcal{N}$OAH

NOAH CAME to an abrupt stop midway between the kitchen and living room, caught between amusement and pain as coffee sloshed from one mug onto his hand. "What happened?" he asked, wincing into the burn from the spilled coffee and trying to unriddle the sight before him. Everly stood in front of the couch, tangled in lights. By the looks of it, Kenobi was caught in the web of Christmas lights too.

"There're *so* many lights," Everly said with a pitiful laugh.

His heart warmed of its own accord at the sight of Everly, but Noah did his best to ignore the feelings that would lead nowhere. Setting the cups on an end table since Kenobi's swishing tail and unpredictable rear end were too near the coffee table, he sized up the situation from a new angle. "Okay. Don't move."

"You're going to untangle me?"

Noah scanned the several strands of lights, spotting at least three plugs—no, four. Some lights twinkled, others blinked, but most didn't work. He could do this; he could remain objective as he unwound the strands from around her body. *Can't I?*

This close it was impossible to miss her alluring vanilla scent. It reminded him of warm summer nights spent stargazing from the tailgate of his truck, Everly tucked against the crook of his arm. "This past summer, I had to help a Morgan who got ensnared in some barbed wire."

"Who's Morgan?"

"Not who. What. Morgan is a breed of horse." He reached for the plug that appeared the easiest to untangle and began weaving it through wires. "Her name was Dolly. She wandered off one morning before a storm. We found her that afternoon with her leg tangled up in the fence. Best we could guess, the thunder startled her so badly she tried to escape."

"That's awful." Everly looked at him expectantly with those big brown eyes. He didn't need to meet her gaze head-on to feel the concern lingering there. "What'd you do?"

"As you can imagine, she was pretty scared. We had to calm her down."

Everly shimmied back a couple of steps, nearly toppling onto the couch. "You're not going to sedate me, are you?"

Noah caught her by the elbow, holding on a few seconds after her legs no longer wobbled. His fingers tingled at the contact. "Thought about it."

"Noah!"

Kenobi let out a bark from the other side of the pile of lights, having wriggled free from the ensnarement on his own. "I'm not *planning* to sedate you," he said with an easy laugh. With mock seriousness, he added, "Unless you start bucking me. Then I might have to reconsider."

"Very funny."

He missed their easy banter more than anything. Everly was easy to rile up over the silliest things. The thought of returning to the ranch left him feeling empty, because her sweet voice would be little more than a memory all over again. "We didn't sedate Dolly, just so you know."

"She had to be dangerous when she was frightened like that. How else do you calm a horse?"

"With soothing words and gentle strokes."

Everly leaned toward him, whether on purpose or subconsciously he couldn't be sure. But his breath grew labored just the same as uninvited feelings reached for the surface.

"That worked?" Everly asked, her words hardly a whisper.

With her lips so close, he could kiss her. Cup her soft cheek with his hand and draw her in until their lips met and reignited the embers of their past into a new and dangerous flame.

Kenobi's head nudged beneath his hand, drawing his attention away with a lick.

"You're going to get all tangled again," Everly said to the dog. "Go look out the window, Kenobi. You're safer over there." The lab licked Everly's hand, still trapped beneath a tangle of lights, and trotted back toward the window.

Noah refocused on the task at hand, successfully freeing one cord—half the lights blinking, the other half dead until he pulled the plug—and starting in on the next. "Reed cut the wire on the fence," he continued his story. "I'll admit, he's a braver man than I am," he added with a laugh. "Dolly's a kicker, even when she's happy."

"Who's Reed?"

"Head foreman at Hope Valley. He runs things now that Uncle Arthur's gone."

"I'm—I'm sorry about your uncle. I didn't know until bingo when the Hartmans—"

"Thank you," he said, working at the second cord. "He's been gone six months now, but it's still hard some days. That ranch was his entire life, and it's not the same without him. He was a tough man, but a good one. He had some good stories." Noah cleared his throat when emotion threatened to surface. "I'm proud to have known and worked for him."

"Is that why you stayed?"

Noah fumbled the cord in his hand. He didn't want to have this conversation right now, or at all if he was being honest. "Part of it."

After he pulled the second cord from the entanglement, Everly was free to use her hands again. Together the two unraveled the remaining strings of lights in seconds. "You could've called me, Noah. Told me you decided to stay. Instead you just— You vanished."

Noah turned toward the coffee cups, buying himself every spare second before he faced her. He tried on a smile, as if whatever she said in response was perfectly okay. "Chloe told me."

Everly frowned, that tiny pinch between her brows still adorable. "Told you what?"

"That you moved on."

"*Two years* later?"

"No, three months after I left." *Three months and eleven days.* He held out her mug until she took it from him. "Chloe told me in one of her weekly emails. Said you started dating some banker from Augusta." Noah pushed aside a pile of garland and sat on the couch.

She hovered where he left her, still holding her mug. "Who are you talking about?"

Noah's heart ceased to beat as he assessed her expression. Genuine confusion lingered in those gentle brown eyes. "I know it was four years ago—"

"Noah, I waited for you for over a year before I finally gave up." Everly eyed the opposite end of the couch but chose to stand in front of the window instead. Kenobi leaned against her leg as she stared out, both hands wrapped tightly around the mug she had yet to take a sip from.

"A year?" The only thing worse than finding out the woman he fell in love with had moved on was finding out that he'd misunderstood the entire situation. Had he really decided to stay in Montana over a simple misunderstanding and ruined their chance at happiness?

"I'm sure that makes me look pathetic. But yes, I waited for a whole year. I thought . . ."

"What?"

"Nothing. It doesn't matter anymore." She turned her back to him and drank her coffee.

The uncomfortable silence made Noah antsy. He fished in his pocket for a phone he rarely carried, not surprised to find it missing. It was probably on his nightstand. He needed to find that email to validate the decision he made to stay. "Then why did Chloe—"

Everly spun back around, causing Kenobi to hop onto all fours. The softness from earlier was gone now, her eyes throwing sparks his way. "I don't know, Noah. Too late for any of this to matter, isn't it? It doesn't change anything. You're still going to leave in a few days." She kicked at a pile of garland in her way and marched out of the room.

From his sanctuary on the couch, Noah listened to the running water in the kitchen, too paralyzed to move.

He'd loved Everly. A part of his heart still held that flame for her. But it didn't change anything, even if he admitted to her that he hadn't moved on either. If he gave up the inheritance, Arthur's grand-daughter had a shot at owning a ranch she hated. He'd promised Reed, and everyone else at Hope Valley, that he wouldn't let that happen. Their fates depended on him.

Despite the overwhelming number of people at bingo last night asking whether he was moving home, staying in Snowy Falls wasn't an option. That much had been crystal clear this morning after a good night's sleep.

The ranch depended on his return.

Everly let out a heavy sigh in the doorway. "We have to get more lights. I didn't find a single strand that lit up all the way. Guess they're all outside."

"Everly, I'm—"

"Let's just get this tree decorated before Annie gets back. We both know it's better this way."

Noah wasn't certain whether she meant keeping Grandma Annie happy or the way things had turned out between them. He didn't ask for clarification. "I'll warm up the truck."

CHAPTER 8

$\mathcal{E}$VERLY

"THERE YOU ARE!" Annie's voice startled Everly from the next aisle over as she leisurely pushed a rickety cart filled with Christmas lights down an aisle of garland. After the unsettling conversation with Noah earlier, she was in no hurry to meet him at the checkout line.

Everly's eyebrows drew in concern at Annie's panicked expression. "Is everything okay?" she asked. Annie hustled around the end display of ornaments and came straight at her. Everly felt both hands tighten on the cart's handle, smooth plastic sliding under her sweaty palms as she twisted. Oh, no. Was it the Taggerts? Chloe? *Mom?*

"Where's Noah?" Annie asked, wasting no time.

"Here," Noah said, appearing beside her.

Everly contained her squeak of surprise this time. Now wasn't the time to chastise him about his uncanny ninja abilities. Her concern over Annie's haste jumbled with remembered thoughts from less than an hour before. *He thought I moved on?*

"What's happened?" he asked.

Annie's eyes filled with worry, hands falling to her hips as she stamped her foot. "Oh, it's positively awful!"

Everly rested her hand on Noah's bicep so automatically she didn't realize what she'd done until tingles skittered up her arm. She blamed it on the cart that trapped him at her side. Immediately, she pulled her hand away and waited for Annie to explain. "Has someone been hurt?" she dared to ask.

"It's Milky Way."

Noah and Everly shared a confused glance, tension from earlier fading as they both tried to understand the emergency.

"Come again?" he asked.

"Milky Way. The horse that's supposed to pull the sled with the mayor in it on Christmas Eve." When neither of them spoke, Annie let out an exasperated sigh. "For the Christmas Eve tree lighting ceremony?"

"What's wrong—"

"Did you find him?" Harold Hartman called

from two aisles over, cutting off Everly's question before she had a chance to finish it. As he approached the ornament display, Everly noticed deep lines pressed across his forehead. He ran a hand over his thinning hair when he stopped. "Noah, we need your help."

Though his stoic expression betrayed nothing, Everly noticed the way Noah fidgeted with the zipper on his coat. A tell, she remembered, that he was silently working to keep anxiety at bay. She only knew because he'd shared this detail with her years ago. One he never shared with anyone.

"What can I do?" he asked.

"Milky Way's limping on her left front leg. It's only gotten worse since the morning. Can I steal you away to take a look? Doc Freeman's out of town for the holidays, and Jim's on the road from Bangor. We can call a vet from Brooksville—"

"No need. I'll come out," Noah said, sounding every bit like the man in charge. Calm, confident, and hyper-focused; different from the man she first fell for, yet in many ways the same. Everly swallowed. He'd been competent before, but still filled with little self-doubts and second guesses. *Maybe the ranch has been good for him after all.*

"Everly, dear," said Annie. "Why don't you go along? They might need an extra set of hands."

Three pairs of eyes fell on her at once. "I think I'd just be in the way," she hedged, backing her cart up a bit to get out of their sight line. "Why don't I go back and get the tree decorated?"

"Annie's right," Harold agreed. "We might need the help. We're shorthanded with the holidays. I'm only covering for Jim as it is, and I don't have to remind you," he said, glancing at Noah, "I don't know much about horses." He laid a hand on the edge of Everly's cart, meeting her eye with something very like a plea. "Better to have too much help than not enough. Noah'll tell us what to do."

"The tree can wait, dear," Annie reassured.

"Where's everyone else?" Everly asked as she and Noah met Harold outside Milky Way's pen. Hartman Horse Farms was one of the biggest establishments of its kind around. She didn't expect it to feel so deserted. She caught a glimpse of a horse standing in the shadows near the barn, but her scan for additional help turned up empty.

"Folks are busy with the main operation." Harold nodded at the massive stable a short walk down a forked drive. "Milky Way has her own accommodations. She's family, you see," Harold explained. "Can't afford to pull anyone away right now, even if they knew what to do."

Noah capped his hand on Everly's shoulder. "It'll be fine, Ev. I need you to help keep her calm.

Soothing words and gentle strokes." He added the last in a low voice that sent shivers throughout her body. Shivers she couldn't blame on the crisp winter air. "You can do this."

She nodded, following the men through the gate. A beautiful caramel and white horse stood at the open entrance to the barn, grunting at their approach. She took a step back, as if she meant to bolt, but froze the instant her weight shifted to the injured leg.

"Easy there, girl." Noah's voice had always possessed that smooth, honey quality to it, but it was even thicker now. "We need to take a look at your hoof. I bet that's what hurts you." Noah slipped off his glove and stroked her neck, his fingertips disappearing beneath Milky Way's thick coat.

"Got a hoof pick, Harold?" Noah asked.

"I'll grab one."

Still stroking Milky Way's neck, Noah looked over his shoulder at Everly. "Come over here," he said, reaching out his free hand in invitation. Without his own gloves, she could feel his strong fingers curl around her own through her mittens. Ignoring the way her heart doubled its beats, she let him lead her to the horse. "See what I'm doing?" he asked, his tone so soft she leaned in to hear him better.

"Yeah."

"Take off your mitten."

Everly slipped them both off, stuffing them in her coat pockets. She let him take her hand again, but this time the brush of his fingers did more than elevate her heart rate. Though Everly had hardly had time to digest their earlier conversation, one thought continued on repeat. *He thought I moved on.*

"I know you've petted a horse before." Up close, the twinkle in his eyes was undeniable. He'd taken her horseback riding on their third date. "Don't go all shy on me now."

Mimicking Noah's strokes along Milky Way's neck was the easy part. Standing this close to the man who once held her heart in the palm of his hands made her shaky. She listened to his instructions over her shoulder, detecting a hint of peppermint on his breath. She smiled fondly at the memory of him dropping a peppermint candy into his coffee on several occasions.

"Got it?" he asked.

"Um, can you repeat that last part?" At least he couldn't see the flush on her face.

"Harold'll hold the reins. I just need you to keep stroking her neck and talking to her. Same way you'd talk to Kenobi if you needed to keep him calm."

"Okay."

"Here's the hoof pick," Harold announced, emerging from the side of the barn with the instrument in hand. Everly's eyes doubled in size at the sight of it. Harold must've caught her panic. "Don't worry," he said to her. "It looks scarier than it is."

"It looks like you robbed Captain Hook of his hand." Noah's low laughter near her ear made her breathe heavier. She tried to calm the reaction, afraid she'd spook Milky Way. Though Everly hadn't spent much time around horses, she did remember they could sense fear. She was here to help, not make things worse. *Get it together, Everly.*

"I'm going to use it to remove the caked dirt," Noah explained, putting her fears to rest. "It's a good practice to keep up with on a regular basis anyway, but that way I can see if she has an abscess."

That doesn't sound good.

"Easy there, Milky Way. Dr. Noah's going to fix you right up." Everly leaned her head against the mare's neck, loving the silky feel of her coat.

"That's perfect, Ev," said Noah. "Got her, Harold?"

"Yep."

Glancing over her shoulder, Everly watched Noah fold Milky Way's leg at the knee and use the hoof pick to remove the caked dirt from inside the hoof. He worked with such ease, the mare swishing her tail in obvious enjoyment. Everly wondered if he handled all the horses at the ranch this way. *I bet he's magnificent out there.*

When Noah told her about his first extension out at the ranch and confessed he wouldn't be home for

Thanksgiving, Everly had toyed with the idea of buying a plane ticket and surprising him. But a mishap with a pothole and the need for a new strut forced her to table the idea. Watching him work, it was easy to wish she'd maxed out her credit card and bought the plane ticket. *Maybe we'd still be together.*

"Looks like she got a rock lodged up there," Noah said. A couple of snorts later and Everly heard the rock thud to the wooden floor. "Got it."

"You did so good, Milky Way," she cooed.

"Yes, you did, girl." Noah rubbed his hand over the mare's muzzle. "Harold did you a favor and called me out here in time. No abscess at all. You're lucky."

"She's okay, then?" Harold asked.

"If I had my bag, I could give her something to ease the pain for today. She'll be sore, but I suspect she'll be good to go for the ceremony. Don't worry too much if she limps the rest of the day, but if she still has trouble in the morning, you'll want to have it checked out."

"Thank you so much, Noah. I know you and Jim—"

"I'm happy to help," Noah said. "I'd feel better coming back out in a couple of days, but I'll leave that up to Jim." Noah gave Harold his cell number. "If I don't hear anything, I won't bother him."

Everly's heart twisted. *He thought I moved on.* Would Noah still have a job at Hartman's Horse

Farms had he known differently? As they walked back to the truck, Everly searched her memories for the banker in Augusta he mentioned. She couldn't think of a single reason Chloe would make something like that up.

Then it hit her.

The lie she'd spun when Chloe tried to set her up on a blind date.

"You did great, Ev," Noah said when they were back in the truck. "You're a real natural with furry creatures. If you weren't such a passionate librarian, I might say you missed your calling. But we both know you didn't."

His words warmed her heart. Never once had Noah thought any less of her because she loved her middle school library and the kids in it. He admired her drive, her passion. More than once, he'd told her that she was his inspiration. And until this moment, she'd forgotten the power of those words.

Sliding his gloves back on, he gave her a sideways smile. "Suppose we have a tree to decorate, don't we?"

"I made it up."

"What are you talking about?"

"The banker from Augusta. Noah, I'm so sorry. I —I just realized why Chloe told you about that. I made it up to dodge one of her setups. I wanted to tell her about us so badly, but we agreed to wait until Christmas."

At the edge of the Hartman's drive, Noah shifted the truck into park and unbuckled his seat belt. Before Everly had a chance to register what was happening, Noah slid over and cupped her cheek. Their eyes locked, so many unspoken emotions, hopes, and dreams lingering there.

"Noah, I'm—"

He leaned closer, pressing his lips against hers. When shock evaporated and memory took over, Everly's lips moved against his, tasting peppermint and coffee. Her body erupted in familiar tingles. His kisses always made her feel a bit like she was flying high above the clouds.

A faint warning whispered in her ear, but Everly pushed it away. She was well aware that kissing Noah Taggert was a terrible idea, but she had no more power to stop it than she did to keep the sun from setting.

$\mathcal{N}$OAH

THE NEXT MORNING, Noah's lips still buzzed from that kiss. When Everly confessed she invented a fake boyfriend to protect their secret and keep Chloe from forcing her on a date, Noah'd been so overcome with surprise and . . . relief. The kiss was a risk, but one he didn't regret taking. It proved the embers still burned for both of them.

That kiss was the sole reason he could smile through the bad news Grandma Annie delivered at the breakfast table.

"They had to reschedule their flight. The so-called groom," Grandma said with air quotes, "has already flown back to New York. But Blakely, well, you know how your sister likes her dramatics." She shook her head, taking a sip of coffee.

Noah nodded. "I guess *that* hasn't changed."

"They don't want to split up, or risk leaving her behind. Heaven forbid she finds *another* man to elope with if they did that." She fussed further with her coffee, adding another spoonful of milk and stirring it with a candy cane. "I have a bad feeling about this, Noah. They should've hog-tied that girl and tossed her on the plane last night. With the storm coming, they won't make it all the way back to Maine without delays. I hate to think of them stranded at an airport for Christmas. That's no way to spend the holidays."

The eagerness to get on a flight of his own slipping away, Noah had to admit he did yearn to see his family. Their absence from all his favorite haunts was an oddity he hadn't grown used to, nor did he want to. Though he wasn't convinced there was a mysterious storm coming, for the first time he didn't feel guilty about spending a few extra days in town. Hope Valley could and *would* manage until his return. What he needed was time with Everly. Noah gulped his coffee. *And a way to sort out a possible future together.*

He nodded, smiling for Grandma. "Let's hope the storm holds out."

Grandma Annie patted him on the arm. "I know you don't believe me now, but you will by sunrise tomorrow." A landline phone rang, drawing Annie to the opposite end of the kitchen. "Why don't you go see if Everly's up?" she asked, reaching for the receiver. "I'm making omelets this morning. With *bacon*."

"That'll do the trick." Noah chuckled with an amused shake of his head. Nerves and eagerness intertwined as he headed downstairs to Everly's room. They hadn't been able to steal a moment alone since that kiss, to talk *about* that kiss or to try out a few more. Last night, Grandma Annie had them busy stuffing stockings and wrapping gifts until Everly was yawning so much her eyes watered.

He wondered if she'd let him steal a kiss this morning.

Her door sat open a crack, a sniffing nose wedged in it halfway up. "Hey, Kenobi," he greeted in a soft tone. The lab's tail thunked against the dresser as he nudged the door all the way open and burst out into the hallway, demanding pats and ear scratches.

"Everly?" He caught her hunched over a book on the bed, her folded legs clad in fuzzy purple, her elbows pressed against her knees. With her auburn hair pulled into a bun, it was easier to spot the earbuds. Noah stole a minute to watch her, fascinated by how intently she was absorbed in the last few pages of her paperback.

The main house at the ranch had a room lined with built-in bookshelves and not nearly enough books to fill them. An image flashed through his mind of Everly tucked into the window seat, engrossed in a novel. *Could she be happy there?*

Kenobi jumped when Everly slammed her book down on the mattress. "Ugh! Stupid cliffhanger." She yanked the earbuds out of her ears and tossed them on the nightstand. "Kenobi, are you—" Her chocolatey brown eyes grew twice their size when she spotted Noah in the hallway, stroking Kenobi's neck.

"Breakfast'll be ready shortly. I'm told there will be bacon."

"I was just reading—"

"Good book? Or not, judging by your reaction."

"*Very* good book. But the darn thing ends on a cliffhanger and the next book isn't due out for another six months. They just kidnapped the hero! Dust bunnies, I don't know if I should get this book or wait until the next in the series is out. My kids might protest if they have to wait that long to find out what happens to Charity. But then again, it's *such* a good book. How could I keep it from them? I should probably get a second copy."

His chest warmed at the way she called them her kids. "Buy two."

"Good idea." She grabbed her phone. "I'll just get them on their way now, before I forget."

"Everly?"

"Yeah?" she asked without looking up.

"Bacon, remember?"

He watched her type in a few commands, press a couple of buttons, then set her phone back on its charger. "Done."

"You kids coming?" Grandma Annie called from the top of the stairs, making Noah feel as if the two of them were up to no good. Kenobi dashed down the hall, taking the staircase in three strides.

"Coming," Noah called back, disappointed that stealing a kiss would have to wait a little longer. He'd only been thinking about it all night long. "Better be quick," he said with a wink.

For the past couple of years, Noah had considered his heart dormant when it came to love. After he accepted that things with Everly were really over, he didn't let himself lie awake at night dwelling on a woman. The rare dates he'd entertained simply for the sake of moving on left him feeling even emptier. He thought about the horses instead. The chores. The inventory. Anything and everything but the prospect of finding love again. Of dwelling on *the* woman he still longed for.

But last night, it'd taken half the night to fall asleep. It wasn't only the kiss on replay, or the way his fingertips tingled in remembrance of her soft skin. It was the idea of a second chance he never thought they'd have.

"We have an emergency on our hands," Grandma Annie said as Noah and Everly entered the kitchen. Her words were calmer than yesterday in the store, but the seriousness in her eyes was just the same.

"What is it?" Everly asked, slipping into her seat at the table. Kenobi trotted over. Instead of commandeering his normal spot beside her chair, he licked her hand, whipped around, and dropped beside Noah.

Noah flashed her a victorious smile, hidden from Grandma Annie.

"Traitor," she mouthed at the lab, though her gaze flickered up to his.

"Thelma Mason came down with the flu," Grandma Annie said. "Isn't that just awful?"

Noah and Everly shared a lingering glance, both trying to dissect the meaning behind the fragment. A sick friend didn't make the emergency any clearer. Noah risked an arched brow. *You got any ideas?*

Everly tilted her head in a nearly unseen *No.* "Right before Christmas?" she said, attempting to draw more details from Grandma Annie. "That *is* awful."

"Poor thing is just beside herself. She volunteered to bake eight dozen sugar cookies for the Christmas Eve tree lighting ceremony," Grandma Annie explained. "Obviously she can't do that anymore."

Noah didn't need to ask questions to know where this was going. "We're never going to get that tree decorated, are we?" he said quietly to Everly, winning a flirty smile that illuminated those beautiful eyes. Their secret exchanges across the kitchen table made him buzz with an emotion he couldn't quite pinpoint, but it felt a bit like hope.

"We'll get everything set up as soon as we finish with the breakfast dishes," Everly offered.

"Oh, good! Her son, John, is going to drop off all the ingredients and cookie cutters shortly. I have enough mixing bowls and cookie sheets to feed the Taggerts on any given holiday." Grandma Annie returned to the stove and began cracking eggs. "Between the three of us, we should be able to knock them out by mid-afternoon. We just have to get them finished before the wind picks up."

Three of us. Noah hid his disappointment behind his lifted coffee mug. He and Everly still had things to sort out—not only about their past misunderstanding, but about their future. He met her gaze over his cup, his heart swelling. Four years ago, he'd been ready to marry Everly. He might be again.

"Still think that storm's coming?" Everly asked.

Grandma Annie cracked a final egg into the pan. "I *know* it is, dear. We'll lose power before the night's over, so better add a couple blankets to your bed tonight. Better yet, you might want to camp out on the couch."

"Grandma Annie," said Noah, leaning back in his chair to better aim his trick question. "If there's a storm coming, will there even *be* a Christmas Eve tree lighting ceremony?"

"Of course there will," she answered as nonchalantly as if he'd asked about lunch. "That tradition is decades old, you know. The storm'll be calmed down by then." Grandma Annie stopped fiddling with the pan and looked straight at Everly. "Noah doesn't believe me about the storm. But mark my words, it'll be here before you know it."

"Did Chloe make it back yesterday with her new rescue?" Noah asked, eager to change the subject away from the mythical storm.

"Oh, no, she's stuck in some small town south of Bangor. Trouble with the van." Grandma Annie shook her head. "She thinks it'll be fixed today, but if they don't get it done soon . . . "

"Why don't I turn on some Christmas music?" Everly suggested, hopping up from her seat. Noah admired her ability to intervene so effortlessly. He wondered if she learned the technique with her students in the library. "If we're going to make a hundred cookies, we better get in the spirit."

"I'll get out the mixing bowls . . . and things," Noah volunteered.

"I'm so lucky to have both of you here to help me," Grandma Annie said, grabbing Noah's arm as he whisked by. "Wouldn't mind that more often than every fourth Christmas."

He slid his arm about her waist, dropping a kiss

to the top of her snow-white hair. "Love you, too, Grandma," he said.

Grandma Annie stared up at him for a long moment, only returning to her omelets when the sizzle demanded attention.

Feeling her gaze upon him, Noah glanced back at Everly, catching her smile. They shared a lingering glance of their own, this one not so secret or short. No, this one held promise. *Hope.*

CHAPTER 10

*E*VERLY

"Wow, WE DID IT, KIDS!" Grandma Annie clapped her hands, her excitement giving way to relief, and a yawn only a moment later. The dishes were washed and put away, the counters wiped cleaned, and the last of the cookies boxed and ready to go. "Eight dozen cookies, plus four more for good measure. I'm pooped!"

Everly slipped into her coat and boots. "I can't believe I'm saying this, but I'm a little bit over cookies."

"Cookies or cookie *dough?*" Noah accused. More than once, he caught her pilfering a stray chunk of sugar cookie dough. Despite his warnings, she couldn't stop herself. Now, all she had to show for it was a mild stomachache and no appetite for dinner.

"You two can handle the delivery, right?" Annie asked, another yawn escaping.

"We got it, Grandma. Go grab a nap. You earned it."

"A short one. Want to be on my toes for tonight. Kenobi, you better come with me. Can't have you helping yourself to the goods." The dog looked back and forth between Everly with her coat on and Annie heading toward her bedroom. "I have *care-ots*," she sang out.

That made up his mind.

Nervous butterflies erupted in Everly's stomach as they carried the Saran-wrapped boxes of cookies, all individually frosted and decorated, out to the truck. Since that kiss yesterday, they hadn't had a single moment alone. At first, Everly had welcomed their distractions. She needed time to think. Time to decide whether kissing Noah had been wise or a mistake.

She still hadn't reached a conclusion.

But time had made one thing clear: she still had feelings for Noah. *Strong* feelings.

"Think we've got them all," Noah said, closing the back door of his truck. He lingered a moment, as if he wanted to say something. Or maybe reach for her hand. Everly would be lying if she claimed she hadn't been thinking about another kiss all after-noon. *But in the driveway?*

A single snowflake fell onto the tip of her nose. "Huh, what do you know?"

They both looked around. "A few snowflakes doesn't mean a blizzard," Noah countered, scanning the overcast sky. But the confidence from the times he doubted the storm wasn't as strong. "But who am I to say?" He shook his head. "I swear, I don't know how she does it."

"Guess we better hurry," she added, disap-pointed that their solo trip would be cut short.

Everly waited until they were a couple of blocks from the house to ask about Milky Way.

"Haven't heard anything," Noah said with a shrug. But his feigned indifference didn't fool her. She wondered what bothered him more, that Jim hadn't called or that he didn't have an invitation to check on a horse he treated.

"You'd still have that job if it weren't for me, wouldn't you? At Hartman's," she added, leaning into the door to look at him better.

Noah stared straight ahead as he drove. "Wasn't meant to be."

Everly frowned, not satisfied with that answer but unwilling to push it. She tried another tactic instead. "I always thought you stayed in Montana because life was more exciting out there than this boring little town."

"Exciting?" Noah shook his head, pulling into a spot outside the community center. The scarce snowflakes from only minutes ago turned puffier and fell quicker, melting against the windshield on impact. "I was busier. Had more responsibility. And some days it felt like more purpose. But that's not why I stayed. I believed you moved on, and I didn't want to get in the way if you'd found someone better. You deserved someone who would be *here*."

Everly's heart melted into a puddle, rendering her unable to operate the door handle now that they'd stopped. "There's never been anyone better, Noah."

Noah's eyes darkened in a way that made her heart flutter. "I could kiss you right now. *Again*."

She wanted him to, but before she could scoot over to make that happen, the front door of the community center burst open and two volunteers rushed out into the snow to retrieve the cookies. *It's for the best*. Kissing Noah, as tempting as that was to repeat, was dangerous. She could guard her heart from the worst of his departure if she stopped more kisses from happening. Staying friends was safer.

But she didn't want to play it safe. She'd been doing too much of that lately.

"You want to put a wager on the tree decorating?" teased Noah, backing out of the parking spot after all the cookies were collected. "I bet twenty bucks Grandma Annie will have something else for us to do when we get back. She might leave it in a note, but there's no way that tree gets a single decoration before tomorrow."

"Twenty bucks? You sound confident."

"I am."

With her gifts all purchased, Everly spent her last bit of fun money on a second copy of a book for her library this morning. But the temptation to slip her hand into his to shake on the wager was too much to resist. "I bet we'll get the whole thing up before bed."

His hand warmed her cold fingers, sending heat up her arm and straight to her chest. *Quicksand*, Mom had warned. Everly didn't doubt she was right.

Kenobi, along with a bare evergreen, filled the picture window when they returned. "Guess *his* nap's over," Noah said.

"Or your grandma ran out of carrots."

Inside, Noah searched the living room and kitchen for a note while Everly watched from the couch, rubbing Kenobi behind the ears. "You're not going to find anything."

"It's here somewhere, I'm sure of it."

"Guess we're getting twenty dollars," Everly said to Kenobi, planting a kiss on his forehead. She reached for the shopping bag filled with the lights they'd purchased yesterday and began unpacking them.

"I'm not admitting defeat," Noah called from the

kitchen. She heard the sloshing of coffee into mugs and the distinct drop of a peppermint against the porcelain. "We have to decorate the *whole* tree," he added, carrying two mugs into the living room with him. "Lights, garland, ornaments, and the angel on top."

"Hope you have cash in your wallet."

"So confident."

"This tree is getting decorated tonight." Everly laid out the strands of lights along the couch, finding it much easier to remain untangled when they were nicely rolled up. She plugged them in one by one, catching a glimpse of the heavier snowfall outside when the howl of the wind drew her attention. *Maybe Grandma Annie's right.*

Noah settled into the couch with his mug in hand, no doubt to help ensure his victory. "You really never dated a banker from Augusta?" he asked.

Everly unwound the first set of twist ties from a rolled-up strand of lights. "No, I didn't." But she recognized the question he was really asking and answered without further prompting. "I dated someone a couple years later, but it never went anywhere." He wanted Everly to move in with him; she wanted out.

"Why not?"

Everly risked the vulnerable answer, despite her constricting throat. "He wasn't you."

Noah rose from the couch, weaving between boxes of ornaments to reach her.

"You're back," Annie said with a yawn, adjusting her glasses.

Everly released a hidden sigh. *Geez*. Maybe fate didn't want them to share a second kiss.

"Hope we didn't wake you. That wasn't a very long nap," Noah said, reaching for the strand of lights Everly had just plugged in and helping her wind them around the base of the tree. He slipped Everly a wink that made the butterflies in her stomach dance like fools.

"Long enough," Annie said. "That howling wind is enough to wake the dead. I'll put on some leftover soup while we still have power."

"What about you?" Everly asked him, Kenobi trotting behind Annie into the kitchen. Working at the twist ties, she studied the new strand of lights in her hand, and cleared her throat of too thick emotions. Keeping her voice low, she added, "You have a lot of girlfriends out at that ranch?"

Noah gave a soft laugh, barely audible above the Christmas music Annie'd turned on. "Nothing worth mentioning. Not a lot of time for that sort of thing out there anyway."

"Really?" Everly raised an eyebrow at him.

"On a good day, Hope Valley is thirty minutes from the nearest town. My social life is a little lacking." Hidden by the tree, Noah took her hand when she passed around another strand of lights. "There's never been anyone else, because no one else has been *you*."

Kenobi's bark from the kitchen was the only thing that kept Everly from shimmying behind the tree and kissing Noah. *Can we make this work?* The question lingered on the tip of her tongue but fear of shattering the moment held it back.

"Hurry up with those lights, now," Annie called above the music. "Soup'll be on in two minutes."

Noah squeezed her hand before he dropped it, but the stolen glances and flirting grazes of their fingers continued as they wound the remaining lights up the tree. Everly found herself whisked away in a fantasy of the two of them decorating their own tree. *Is next Christmas too soon for us to be married?*

Another bark from Kenobi served as the dinner bell.

Everly and Noah helped carry bowls and fixings to the table, and the three had barely scooted into their chairs before the lights flickered for several seconds. They watched the fixture above the table until it went dark for good.

Noah hopped out of his chair to try the switch to no avail. "Grandma Annie, are you psychic?" he asked, less teasing in his voice now and more awe.

"Don't be ridiculous," she chided.

Everly wondered the same, though she didn't speak the words. Not only had Annie predicted the storm, but the power outage as well. *I wonder how she is with lottery numbers?* She hid her smile behind a glass of milk.

Annie stared out the window. "We have enough daylight to finish eating. Then I'll get out the candles."

Returning to his seat, Noah looked over his shoulder at Everly, catching her with a spoon halfway to her lips. "You have that cash handy or do I need to take you to an ATM after dinner?"

She abandoned the spoon to her bowl, a victorious smile pointed at him. "I think you underestimate my determination, Noah Taggert. We're finishing that tree by candlelight."

CHAPTER 11

*N*OAH

A WET NOSE nudged Noah's hand, forcing him to open his eyes. "Hey, Kenobi," he said quietly so as not to disturb a sleeping Everly curled against his chest. The glow of Christmas lights illuminated the otherwise dark room. *Guess the power came back on.*

Thirst begged him to seek out water, but Noah refused to move and disturb the angel he held in his arms. Tucked against his chest, the hint of vanilla shampoo brought him comfort. He remembered a night stargazing in the bed of his truck with that same wonderful scent painting the memory before him.

I want this. Every night.

Noah rubbed his fingers over Kenobi's head, admiring the fully decorated tree. The darker the room grew as the evening fell, the more determined Everly had become to finish it. Noah pretended to stall, but secretly he wanted her to win.

A Christmas tree was the only hint that the holidays were near at the ranch, but their decorations seemed skimpy by comparison. Though the tree at the ranch had a few handmade decorations as this tree did, it lacked the array of shiny ornaments Grandma Annie had collected over the years.

Noah cricked his neck a little, better able to see the glossy ceramic angel ornament he'd gifted Grandma Annie half a dozen years ago. Not far from it was a family of salt dough snowmen. If he remembered right, the trio had been made by Chloe, Blakely, and Libby while he and his brothers strung lights on the tree.

Noah swallowed a lump, emotions squeaking in the tight space. In this isolated moment in time, it was easy to imagine future holidays just like this one. *I bet Everly'd deck the whole ranch out in holiday spirit.* Next Christmas, Noah determined, he was bringing holiday cheer back to the ranch, even if he had to drive six or more hours to find the decorations.

Contentment tugged at him, drifting his attention from one memorable ornament to the next, but the creak of a door down the hall sent alarm through him instead. *Grandma Annie!* As carefully as he could, he shimmied out from beneath Everly, resting her head against a throw pillow.

Grandma Annie found him covering Everly with a blanket.

He didn't want to keep his feelings for Everly a secret from his family. *Not this time.* But he wasn't eager to explain them being cuddled together on the couch in the middle of the night when no one knew a thing.

"Power came back on," he said in low voice to Grandma Annie.

She nodded, but a knowing twinkle danced in her eyes.

Or did they?

"House should be back to temp within an hour," she said as Noah followed her into the kitchen. She turned on the stove light and filled a glass of water.

Noah swallowed, fearing a lecture was on the horizon.

"The tree looks lovely," Grandma Annie said, handing over the glass.

Noah took a slow, cautious sip. "Everly did most of the work," he admitted.

"I like her, Noah. A lot. She's become one of the family, even more so now with her mom on another continent. I'm sure you see that."

I like her, too. Noah kept his thoughts quiet, fearing sabotage. "But?"

Grandma Annie patted him on the arm. "I want

it to work out with you two. I wanted that years ago." The words caught Noah off guard, rendering him unable to cloak his expression. "But you two have some big things to sort out. Things you can't ignore. I don't want her to get hurt again."

Noah didn't know what to say, so he nodded instead.

"Get some sleep. There'll be plenty of snow to shovel in the morning."

He let out a quiet laugh. "I believe you now."

"Goodnight, Noah."

Noah spent the better part of the morning outside with a snow shovel, wishing he had a snowblower. Wind whipped furiously at his face and gloved hands, cutting right through his coat to the bone. The grueling labor did give him time to think.

He couldn't give up the ranch.

He made a promise to everyone there that he'd keep it and protect them from Uncle Arthur's granddaughter. She had to survive a year before she had the option to sell it, but no one doubted she would the first chance she got. The ranch didn't mean anything to the city girl who never visited, no matter how much Arthur wanted to keep it in the family. Noah wished his uncle had willed the ranch to Reed instead, the one man truly worthy of such a place.

But the terms were what they were. *Can I convince Everly to move to Montana?*

He imagined Kenobi running freely, barking at the horses and chasing after birds. They could plant carrots in the garden just for him. The lab would be happy, especially with all the snowfall in the winter months. But Everly would have to sacrifice her school librarian position. Would ranch life and the corner room filled with bookshelves be enough to appease her passion? There weren't any kids living at Hope Valley and hadn't been in years. Even if they started trying right away, it'd be a while before she had a little one to read to.

Noah stuck the shovel into a snowbank, irritated to find the sidewalk he just cleared filled with drifts. "This is pointless," he muttered.

Catching a glimpse of Kenobi in the window made him smile. All he could do was ask Everly to come with him, maybe after the school year was over. They could do the long-distance thing for a few months if they had a plan—a solid one this time.

Noah marched inside, deciding he'd shovel again after the wind died down. "You can't even tell I did anything," he said in defeat, bolting the door behind him to ensure the wind wouldn't catch it. "There's already an inch of snow on the driveway, and drifts all down the walk."

"You don't shovel snow in Montana?" Everly teased from her spot on the couch. She sat cocooned in a blanket, a book spread in her lap. Kenobi curled in a ball beside her, resting his head against her thigh.

He wanted this sight every day.

"Fewer shovels and more bobcats," he answered, checking his Stetson before dropping it over a hook. "Plus there's almost always an animal to tend to when the cold strikes. I usually get out of the snow-related chores."

"Lucky you."

He remembered her warmth in his arms last night and wondered if Everly had any recollection of falling asleep that way. They had to figure this out, today. Deep in the recesses of his heart, Noah never stopped loving Everly. He'd bet the ranch she never stopped loving him either.

"Where's Grandma Annie?"

"Taking a nap. Says she's resting up for the Christmas Eve festivities tomorrow."

"Have you ever been around for one with us Taggerts?" he asked, wondering if she attended them during the years he was gone.

Everly shook her head. "I've heard the stories, though."

"Grandma Annie's smart to rest up. She puts on quite the festive family party." Noah shed his coat and gloves, eyeing a spot on the couch next to Everly. *We'll figure this out.* "That tree looks pretty good, if I do say so myself."

"Coming over to pay up?" Everly teased.

Before heavy conversation of the future, Noah yearned for another kiss. A confirmation that what they both felt wasn't some fluke or nostalgic memory. He no sooner dropped onto the couch before they heard the roar of a machine.

"Snowplow?" Everly guessed.

"Snow something," Noah mumbled, ignoring the noise. He brushed her cheek instead, hooking her chin with his thumb and drawing her closer to his lips. Everly leaned in, closing what little gap remained. Their lips brushed in a soft kiss, as if both were certain they'd be interrupted and need to jump apart without warning.

"It's quiet," Everly said, her voice a breathy whisper. Kenobi groaned his annoyance and hopped off the couch, causing them both to laugh. "Well, except for him."

Noah pressed his lips to hers again, this time with more intent. Her soft fingers snaked around his neck and pulled him closer. Reality slipped away as he found himself lost in her kiss. Had he ever kissed Everly like this before? He felt the future forming before him in a quick flash. In every image, she was smiling at him.

"What was that for?" Everly asked when they finally broke apart, maybe one minute later, or ten.

Noah took her hand in his own. "Because I've thought of nothing else since I kissed you the first time."

"Which first time? Or don't you remember our *first* kiss?" Her brown eyes sparkled, the happiness in them unmistakable.

"Oh, I remember."

"What do you remember?"

"The sunlight in your hair."

"*That's* what you remember?"

"*Shh*, I'm not done. I remember the sunlight in your hair, the way it glimmered and made some of the strands look like gold. Your red-painted nails with paw prints on the thumbs. Your hand in mine as we walked along the beach in Brooksville. The salty smell of the ocean as we stopped to watch the sunset. How your lips tasted like salted caramel."

"You have a good memory." Everly's gaze dropped to his lips, but before she could lean in for another kiss, Kenobi barked.

"He does that a lot," Noah observed.

Everly winked at him, squeezing his hand. "He let us get a couple in this time."

Pounding on the front door interrupted what was left of the moment, followed by someone rattling the doorknob. Noah popped off the couch to undo the deadbolt and opened the door with caution.

"Noah?"

"Lane?"

"You going to let me in or make me freeze?"

Noah noticed a clear driveway and a snowblower sitting off to the side half a second before he jumped out of the way so his oldest brother could come in out of the cold. "What are you doing here?" Noah asked.

"I could ask you the same thing. I thought you were in Montana."

"I thought you were in Cancun."

Kenobi let out a bark, no doubt because their new guest failed to acknowledge him with a head scratch. As soon as Lane removed his gloves, he obliged the excited lab. "Hey there, Kenobi. You behaving yourself, or is Grandma Annie stuffing you too full of carrots?"

"Careful with that word."

"Grandma Annie, you're up," said Noah.

"I took care of your driveway and sidewalks," Lane said.

Noah raised an eyebrow at his brother. "I did that already."

"But I did it right."

"If you two will stop bickering by the front door, I'll put on some coffee," Grandma Annie ordered. "Lane, come on in and tell us how you're in Snowy Falls before the rest of the family."

CHAPTER 12

E VERLY

"THEY SENT me ahead to check on things," Lane explained to the group gathered around Annie's kitchen table. Everly had to admit she'd miss this table when she moved out. She spent more time here than anywhere else in the house. "Wish someone had told me Noah was already here."

"I wanted it to be a surprise," Annie interjected. "Thought your mother might appreciate that."

The Taggert men exchanged knowing nods. Their mother, Robyn, was known as the queen of surprises, but it was tricky to surprise *her*. "Hope Chloe didn't spill the beans," Noah said.

"I asked her *not* to include your unexpected

arrival in any family updates." Annie stirred her candy cane in a cup of coffee she'd yet to sip. "She's still stuck in that little town; can't quite remember the name of it. Forgot her phone charger, wouldn't you know."

No wonder my texts are going unanswered. "How is she calling you?" Everly was too curious not to ask. More than anything, she wanted her best friend's advice. No made-up dates or secrets anymore. She vowed complete honesty with Chloe, and desperately wanted her advice on how to navigate the challenging waters ahead.

"She borrowed someone's phone," Annie said dismissively, no doubt eager to return to more important topics. Like why Lane was the only Taggert back from Cancun. "She's giving a soldier a ride home and is in good hands. I know she'll make it back for the tree lighting."

Though Annie had a knack for being right about a lot of things, that ability seemed heightened these past few days. *Christmas magic?* Everly wished for a little of that for herself. Maybe then, Noah might consider moving home.

"Anyway," Lane continued after a quick sip of coffee. "We knew one of us needed to come home early; check on house plants, pick up mail, and relieve the neighbors of Tango sitting. So..."

Noah smirked. "Lost rock, paper, scissors with Will, didn't you?"

Lane glared over the rim of his mug, answering with a shrug.

"Where is Tango anyway?" Noah asked.

"Passed out at Mom and Dad's. Poor guy was overstimulated from that cat. I don't think he slept a wink the whole time we've been gone."

"And what about Blakely?" Annie asked.

"She's throwing a tantrum in true Blakely fashion. Convinced her family ruined her life and all that. You'd think she was fifteen instead of twenty-two." Lane took a long sip. "I think she's just too embarrassed to come home. She'll no doubt have to cancel her social media accounts to avoid virtual shame."

"Think they'll make it home in time for Christmas?" Everly asked.

Lane fished his phone out of a shirt pocket and flipped through a few screens. "Flights are all on time so far. If everything stays on track, they'll be back tomorrow evening. But this storm . . ." He let his words taper off and all eyes pivoted to Annie.

She lifted her hands. "Don't look at me. I don't have a crystal ball, you know."

"You sure about that?" Noah asked with a raised eyebrow.

"What brought you back?" Lane asked Noah. "Surprise visits aren't really your thing. Lose a bet?"

Watching the interaction between the two of them made Everly wish she had siblings of her own.

Her house had been eerily quiet growing up in comparison to the Taggert household. She'd always longed for a sister or brother to rile up.

"Uncle Arthur wanted me to spread some of his ashes in Snowy Fall this week. Wants the whole family present."

Lane nodded, lifting his mug to his lips. "You weren't going to stay for Christmas, were you?"

"As the primary vet, I'm kinda needed at the ranch. Every day I'm gone, the vet down the road has to cover. She's too busy on her own as it is."

Everly frowned at the words, but she couldn't pinpoint whether it was because Noah admitted he never meant to stay longer than he had to, or because the neighboring vet was a woman. Jealousy wasn't an emotion she felt often, and she didn't care for it now.

"Who's running things now that Arthur's gone anyway?" Lane asked.

"I am."

Everly choked on his admission and her coffee.

"You okay, dear?" Annie asked from across the table.

"Yep." Kenobi dropped his head in her lap as she coughed and reached for water. "Sorry, wrong pipe." Despite Noah's lingering gaze, she avoided looking back at him. She had no idea he was running an entire ranch. That . . . changed things.

"What do you know about running a ranch anyway?" Lane picked up the conversation as if it'd never been interrupted. "You're a vet, not a ranch owner. Wait. Did Uncle Arthur leave *you* the ranch?"

"Noah, is this true?" Annie asked.

Kenobi licked Everly's hand until she ran her fingers along the back of his head. Whether the motion was to appease her dog or soothe herself, she wasn't sure. But she was grateful Kenobi always appeared when she needed him most. *At least I can count on* him.

"It's complicated," Noah answered. "But yes is the short answer."

Everly's heart hammered in her chest, unable to process what all this meant—except that Noah wouldn't be moving home. *He couldn't.* "Will you excuse me?" She scooted out of her chair. "I have a few gifts to finish wrapping. I'll let you three finish catching up."

"Of course, dear," Annie said. "If you're free this afternoon, maybe you could help with the pumpkin pies?"

"I can help you, Grandma," Noah interjected, reminding Everly how much the man *loved* his holiday dessert. He once told her he'd rather have a pumpkin pie on his birthday than any flavor cake.

"You can *both* help," Annie said with a laugh, waving Everly free.

Everly hurried down the stairs so quickly she beat Kenobi to their room. The lab lingered in the doorway, tail swishing slowly and head cocked. He was probably wondering if she *really* needed him or if it was safe to return to the kitchen and wait for snacks.

Everly desperately wished she could talk to her mom. The conversation would certainly include an I-told-you-so lecture, but she craved it just the same. Without much hope, she flipped open her laptop and logged into her Skype account.

"She's not online, buddy," she said to Kenobi who'd joined her on the bed and rested his head against her thigh. "And Chloe doesn't have any battery. Guess her phone will explode once she gets to plug it in."

The memory of the kisses they shared less than an hour ago tangled with the new information that Noah *owned* the ranch.

Gentle knocking turned her head.

"Can I come in?" Noah asked, poking his head through the door.

She wanted to say no, but Kenobi's tail thumped against the bed at Noah's voice. Everly turned to face him, running her fingers through the dog's amber fur to ground herself. *I can do this. No more misunderstandings.* "Why didn't you tell me?"

"I was going to," Noah said, shutting the door behind him and risking Grandma Annie's wrath if she should come downstairs and find them on the other side of a closed door together.

"When? *After* you went back to Montana?"

Noah sat on the opposite edge of the bed. Kenobi combat-crawled on his stomach until he reached him, offering his head for rubbing and leaving Everly with his butt. *Of course, Kenobi.*

"Believe it or not, right before Lane pounded on the door." Noah let out a heavy sigh, thawing the icy wall she'd fortified moments ago. He reached for her hand, and against her better judgment, she let him take it. "I only kept it from you because I didn't think it mattered. But I promise, once I knew"—he paused, drawing a shaky breath though his gaze never wavered—"I was going to tell you everything."

"What changed?"

"We kissed."

Everly softened a little more. "You don't think your grandma would want to know you inherited a ranch? That's kind of a big deal. I'm guessing you haven't told anyone or Chloe would've alerted the entire family."

"It's conditional."

"What is?"

"The terms of the inheritance," Noah explained. "I have to work there a year, learn every aspect of running a ranch, way beyond the responsibilities of a vet. If I don't pass the test, the same conditions go to the next family member on the will."

"Who?"

"Arthur's granddaughter."

Everly sought to understand, but couldn't put the pieces together on so little information. "Why is this a bad thing?"

"She hates the ranch. She'd sell it the first chance she got, and lifelong employees would lose their jobs. They have families to support. I can't let them down. Running a ranch is hard work, but I have one of the best managers there is. He does most of the heavy lifting."

"Reed?" Everly guessed.

"Yep."

"Where does that leave us, Noah?"

He squeezed her hands, drawing her attention downward. Her red nails had Christmas trees on the thumbs. A detail she'd always remember when she thought about Noah and this moment. "Come to Montana with me."

"What?" Everly felt certain she'd heard him wrong.

"You'd love the ranch. You're good with the horses, and Kenobi would have so much room to run. There's even a neglected library in the main house that could use a booklover's touch."

Everly had to admit the offer sounded more enticing by the second. "But the library. I can't leave my kids, Noah. Not in the middle of a school year."

He wriggled one hand free to cup her cheek, tilting her face up until she met his gaze. "Come to Montana after the school year ends. We can make the long-distance thing work until then. I'll even fly home for a couple of long weekends in between. We're not the same people we were four years ago, Ev."

The room felt as if it were spinning, and Everly couldn't keep her eyes from dropping to Noah's lips. The impulsive, reckless side of her wanted to leap at this chance of a life with Noah. The same part of her that was through playing it safe. But the sensible side that would never make such a rash decision on a whim was not to be silenced. "Can I think about it? It's just so life-altering."

"Of course."

Everly thought he might kiss her again; she'd never turn *that* down. But Annie's voice hollered down the stairs. "Noah, are you down there? You have a phone call."

"Wonder who that is," he said, hopping off the bed and jerking the door open in case Grandma was on her way down. "Coming," he called to Annie.

Everly tiptoed to the door, unable to sate her curiosity by hiding in her bedroom. "C'mon, Kenobi. I promise I'll find you a carrot."

"It's Jim Hartman," she heard Annie say, but the rest of the words were lost among the swirl of her own thoughts.

It was too much to hope that Noah would find his purpose—his happiness—in Snowy Falls. Even if Mr. Hartman's call was a job offer, she felt certain

Noah would decline. It was one thing to walk away from a position that could be easily refilled, but quite another to walk away from a ranch and the people depending on it for their livelihoods.

"What do you think, Kenobi?" she asked the lab at the foot of the staircase. "Think you'd like Montana?"

CHAPTER 13

$\mathcal{N}$OAH

"Thanks for coming out on Christmas Eve," Harold said to Noah, extending his hand for a shake.

"No problem. I'm happy to check on Milky Way and make sure she's up to the task tonight." Already he could see that the mare was trotting around her pen without a hint of a limp. This checkup should be quick. He scanned the barn for signs of his former boss, only mildly surprised to find him absent. "Jim around?"

"Out in the main stable," Harold said. "Asked me to meet you."

Noah nodded, not surprised that Jim would avoid him even after requesting he come out this morning. Noah wanted to apologize in person, not over a phone call. Maybe his decision to hold off until today had been unwise.

"Where's your girl?"

Noah did like the sound of that. *My girl.* "Back at Grandma Annie's, helping prepare the Taggert feast." He'd considered inviting her, but Grandma Annie didn't give him the chance. He was doing his best to give her the space she needed to make her decision, but it was harder than he'd bargained. Tomorrow night he'd board a plane and, one way or another, his life would be changed.

"Your family going to make it in?"

"Lane already snuck in on us." Noah filled Harold in on the surprise visitor as he examined Milky Way's hoof, relieved to find everything in order. No abscess, no swelling, no redness, no heat. "He says the rest of the family got on their flight last night. Been tracking them with some app."

"Amazing what a phone can do these days, isn't it?"

Noah had no opposition to technology, but he did enjoy how little he was able to lean on his phone out on the ranch. Still, the prospect of returning to Montana and having to rely on that phone, and his spotty service, to stay in touch with Everly made him frown. *It'll only be for a few months*, he reasoned with himself. *If she agrees to come to Montana at all.*

"Noah Taggert, as I live and breathe, I didn't

think you were ever going to leave Arthur's ranch." Jim Hartman leaned against the fence, adjusting his ball cap. "Sorry to hear about your uncle's passing."

Noah nodded his thanks. "Milky Way's good to go," he told Jim, rubbing the mare along the neck one last time before slipping his gloves back on. It was too much to hope for a thank you. Jim wasn't really that type of man.

"What do I owe you?" Jim asked.

Noah waved away the question as he unlatched the gate and slipped out of the pen, Harold behind him. "Merry Christmas."

"You moving back to town, then?" Jim asked.

"No. Just home for a few days."

Jim pushed off the fence, adjusted his hat, then stuffed both hands in his coat pockets. "Well, if you do make it out this way again, stop over."

Is that a job offer? "Will do."

"See you tonight at the tree lighting," Harold added as Noah headed to his truck. The brothers turned heels, striding toward the main stable before Noah could extend an official apology to Jim. If he wasn't mistaken, that fence was now mended.

Leaving Hope Valley to chance wasn't something Noah could do, but it did bring him comfort to know he hadn't burned the bridge with Hartman Horse Farms to ash as he thought.

❧

EVERLY

EVERLY CRAVED A NAP.

Preparing Christmas Eve dinner for the Taggerts was no joke. Annie put her to work first thing that morning peeling enough potatoes to feed every kid in her elementary school twice. The mashed potato production alone was a full-time job. Add in the turkey *and* ham, two pans of green bean casserole, homemade stuffing, candied yams, and cranberry salad—Everly was dead on her feet.

And dishes. *So many dishes.*

Even Kenobi had tired of the work, curling up on the rug under the kitchen table an hour after they began. He was only awake now, dramatically stretching his way toward them, because his hope for handouts during their quick break was high.

"I'm sure glad we made those pumpkin pies last night," Everly said to Annie as they moved to the table, sneaking an overdue lunch. Staying busy with her hands, conversation nearly impossible with the constantly running mixer, gave her time to think about Noah's offer. To consider life in Montana. *It would be different.* Everly scratched Kenobi behind the ears. But they'd be together—the three of them.

"I've got this production down to a science." Annie gave her a wink. "But I'm sure grateful for your help this year."

"You don't usually do this alone, do you?"

"Years ago I did. But now, Robyn volunteers one of the kids as tribute. I suspect that's the real reason they stayed another night in Cancun. Sure glad everyone is on their way. At last report, Lane said only one flight in their itinerary had a delay."

Everly would miss this kitchen table perhaps more than anything else, except her library and her students. She'd snuck up to the office last night and searched online for librarian jobs near the ranch, not surprised her search turned up empty. She searched for *any* jobs and was disappointed to find very little, and nothing within her skill set.

But she didn't have family of her own in Snowy Falls. No ties outside of friends and a job she loved. Maybe she could earn her keep working on the ranch, and spend her evenings nestled in that home library Noah mentioned.

"A penny for your thoughts?" Annie asked.

Everly bought herself a few seconds, leisurely chewing on a bite of broccoli and cheddar casserole. It'd feel as if a burden were lifted to talk to *someone* about her dilemma. "Any word from Chloe?"

Annie's penetrating gaze warned Everly the woman wasn't fooled. "They're waiting for the roads to be cleared, but the snow stopped dumping on them. I expect her back this evening."

"Good. That's good."

Annie covered Everly's hand with her own and

waited until Everly looked up at her. "There's more than one solution to every problem." She squeezed her hand before letting go and clearing the table. "We still have to tackle the corn and bake some cookies."

"*More* cookies?"

"Only one batch this time. You're lucky I baked the spritz cookies after Thanksgiving and froze them." Annie took Everly's plate from her and rinsed it off in the sink. "I promise after the cookies, you're free to go."

Everly wasn't sure what did it exactly, but a wave of emotion swept through her. She wrapped both arms around Annie and held on tight. "Thank you, Annie."

"Whatever for?"

"For . . . everything?"

"You're family, Everly. No matter how everything turns out."

CHAPTER 14

$\mathcal{E}$VERLY

KENOBI TUGGED ON HIS LEASH, pulling at Everly a bit as they walked along the crowded downtown strip. The road was closed to traffic and as a result, the street was lined with half the town. Every year was the same—the laughter of children, the aroma of coffee from Maine Street Bean cupped in dozens of hands, scarves and hats as far as the eye could see. Giant wreaths hung from the light posts, and most businesses had holiday displays lighting up their windows.

This was the first year Everly was attending without Mom but, to her surprise, the magic held just the same. Besides, there'd be Noah once she found him. He'd been pulled away all day, first at Hartman's, then by his brother. Not surprising, she missed him. It left her to wonder how she'd handle another round of long distance.

Could I really give this up? Everly took in every decoration, detail, and smiling face as she allowed Kenobi to lead the way closer to the massive evergreen planted in the center of town. *Or would we come back every Christmas to visit?*

"Everly!" Chloe's excitable voice rang above the low hum of conversation. She flung her arms around Everly before she had a chance to properly brace herself for impact. Her legs teetered but stayed upright.

"I'm so glad you made it back. I was worried."

Chloe crouched down, giving Kenobi a proper, full-on hug greeting. "In the nick of time, too." She popped to her feet and scanned the crowd.

"Heard you had some troubles with the van," Everly said, following the path of Chloe's search but turning up empty.

"Alternator, wouldn't you know?" The beaming smile left Everly confused, as she expected tired eyes and a series of yawns after what she assumed was a long, rough few days with a rambunctious dog stranded in an unfamiliar town. "It's all good now."

"Lane's here already," Everly told her. "Grandma Annie's back at the house, preparing for *the feast*. But I haven't heard anything on the rest of them yet. They should be getting in tonight." *And Noah . . .* Everly yearned to make her confession while the two had a moment alone. No more secrets between best friends.

"That's all good news. Really good news." Chloe's distracted nature and indifference to her family's whereabouts rose Everly's eyebrow.

"Searching for someone?"

Chloe squeezed both of Everly's arms, finally looking at her. "Do you believe in Christmas magic?"

"I think I'm starting to."

Chloe nodded toward a tall, broad-shouldered man in an Army uniform. A black and white dog— some mix of husky and shepherd, if Everly were to guess—stood by his side, tail wagging enthusiastically. His back was turned toward them. "Is that the man you gave a ride to?"

"Sure is."

"Belle's new owner?"

"Not exactly," Chloe hedged, shifting from one foot to the other. But before she could elaborate, a gaggle of people surrounded them. The entire Taggert clan, minus Noah and Annie, stood around them in a half circle. Even Blakely, though her disgruntled frown made it clear she was only attending the tree lighting by force.

Halfway through the exchange of hugs and welcome backs, everyone's attention fixed on someone behind Everly. "Is that . . . *Noah?*" Robyn covered her agape mouth with a hand. "It can't be—"

"Hey, Mom." Noah's suave, honey voice still made butterflies act up in Everly's stomach. She wondered if they always would. More than that, Everly feared they'd stop completely if she let Noah go a second time and didn't make the decision to go with him.

As the Taggert clan descended on Noah, Everly caught a tiny hand waving at her near the tree. She slipped away to greet one of her students. "Hey, Timmy!" She exchanged smiles with Timmy's mom, Angela.

"Sorry to pull you away," Angela said. "Timmy insisted he had to talk to you."

"Not at all."

"Ms. Jensen, I finished *both* books already."

"That's wonderful." Everly bent over, bringing her closer to eye level with the eleven-year-old. "Which one did you like the best?"

Timmy took off like a bottle rocket, talking so fast about horses, a mischievous little boy, and endless adventure that Everly could hardly keep up. His excited words warmed her heart. Timmy had given her quite the challenge when it came to finding him not just one—but two—books for the break. He read voraciously, and finding books he both liked and hadn't read kept her busy on the hunt for a week.

"I'm so glad you liked it, Timmy. I had a feeling

you would." Before Everly could stand, another student—Bethany—ran right at her, wrapping her in a hug. Kenobi barked enthusiastically, winning some pets from Timmy.

Minutes later, half a dozen students surrounded her, all excitably talking about the books they loved. She fought a single tear that threatened to make an appearance, uncertain how she'd ever be able to leave them behind.

But one glance at Noah, flashing her a helpless smile from the middle of his family, and she knew she loved him. Distance would never change the way her heart felt. As hard as it would be to leave everything behind, she couldn't imagine her life without Noah in it. Not anymore.

～

NOAH

NOAH STOOD ON THE SIDEWALK, hands stuffed in his coat pockets, as his siblings and Mom talked on top of one another. As if everyone wanted to update him on the last four years all at once. Except Dad, who took the same stance and offered a pitying smile and helpless shrug.

But all the words were lost as Noah's attention traveled across the town square to where Everly stood surrounded by the kids she called her own. The excitement illuminating every small face was nothing compared to the glow Everly wore on her own.

"I know you love her." Chloe bumped against his shoulder, keeping her voice low. "But you can't ask her to leave, Noah. That's not fair to her."

It didn't matter anymore *how* Chloe came to figure out his feelings for Everly. Only that she was right. It'd been easy to forget her passion when they were cooped up in the house on holiday break. But seeing her at the ceremony with those kids she adored was something else. "The ranch—"

"It wasn't fair of Uncle Arthur to put that responsibility on your shoulders, either."

Chloe looped her arm through Noah's and discreetly tugged him away from the chattering family. They'd started arguing about some event in Cancun and didn't seem to notice Noah ducking out.

"What am I supposed to do?" he asked Chloe.

"Can't answer that."

"Gee, you're helpful tonight."

"Have a little faith. What is it that Grandma Annie always says? There's always more than one solution to any problem?"

Noah only wished he knew what those were.

CHAPTER 15

$\mathcal{N}$OAH

DESPITE THE HEAVINESS weighing Noah down all through Grandma Annie's Christmas Eve feast, he enjoyed the busy chatter of his family. The way his siblings bickered and ganged up on each other. Their laughter and smiles. He'd *missed* them.

It was easy enough to pretend otherwise when he worked from sunup to sundown at the ranch. But now, with them bombarding him as though he were a celebrity, he already hated the thought of leaving them behind so soon. If Reed hadn't sent him an email, not two hours ago, asking for a reminder on how they tricked Peaches to take her powdered supplement, he might've extended his stay a few more days.

Yes. Hope Valley needed him.

"You sure someone else can't run that ranch?" Grandma Annie asked, wrapping an arm around him and squeezing him in a side hug. "It was really wonderful having you home this year."

"I'll make it back for more holidays. I promise." He offered a smile, but it was forced at best. The assessing gleam in Grandma Annie's eyes said she knew it, too. "You can always come out to Montana for a visit," Noah offered.

"I've done my traveling." She patted him on the arm before darting off to the next task.

He needed to talk to Everly, without a mob listening in. But he'd been denied every opportunity at the tree lighting ceremony. There was always *someone* around. But she had to know something was up because the one time she reached for his hand, seconds before the evergreen shone to life, he shoved his hands in his coat pockets.

It was the reason, he was certain, Everly kept slipping in and out of the gathering. He searched the living room for her again, coming up empty aside from Kenobi who was more than happy to get as many pats as he could. *Must be downstairs*. It didn't make the conversation they needed to have any easier to digest.

"Grandma Annie, when do we get to have

pumpkin pie?" Libby begged, drawing an amused smile out of Noah. Distracting him a few minutes more.

"After we open presents, like every other year. Patience, child."

"Can I sneak a piece? Pretty please?" Libby's bell earrings jingled with her pleas.

Noah laughed at Grandma Annie's expression that said it all, sending his sister bolting out of the kitchen. "Had to try," Libby said in passing.

"We wearing you out yet?" Mom bumped her shoulder into his arm.

"I've always wondered how you handled all of us," he said, draping an arm around her shoulder and pulling her against him. "But now I think you should've won an award."

"Or at least an all-expenses-paid vacation that does *not* involve rescuing one of my kids from stupidity. Do you really have to fly back tomorrow night?"

"Afraid so."

"Well, don't make any plans tomorrow before you leave. After we scatter Uncle Arthur's ashes, I have plans for you." Mom slipped out of his hold and headed for a rare empty spot on the couch before someone else claimed it.

With presents at least twenty minutes away, Noah took the opportunity to slip downstairs unnoticed. The chatter of conversation faded as he made his way to Everly's room. Her door was closed, and

Noah wished he didn't have to knock on it. Not with this news. But Chloe was right. He couldn't ask her to give up what she loved most to move back to a ranch he was only keeping out of obligation. Noah loved Hope Valley, but he wished more than anything that Arthur hadn't stuck him in such a tight corner.

"Hey, Ev?"

"Hey." She smiled at him, but it didn't reach her eyes. No doubt she already suspected something was wrong.

"Can we talk?"

Everly nodded, waiting for him to sit on the opposite side of the bed. Again, he closed the door, now risking the wrath of several Taggerts instead of only one. But this private conversation didn't need any eavesdroppers.

"I was going to say yes, you know." It was now that Noah noticed the blurriness in her pretty brown eyes. She swiped at a tear with the sleeve of her sweater.

Noah felt his heart crack in two. "I can't let you do that."

"Why?"

The overwhelming urge to pull her into his arms and hold her tight tugged at him, but he fought the impulse. He didn't need to make this harder than it already was. "I can't ask you to give up what you love most. It's not the books themselves. It's the kids whose lives you impact. I saw you in town, with the kids. You were lit up brighter than any Christmas tree. So were they."

"They'll all grow up and leave me anyway. They always do."

"Can you honestly say you wouldn't miss them? Miss your library?"

Everly bit her lip, looking away to the stack of books on her desk.

Noah drew a steadying breath. "Hope Valley, well, it doesn't have that opportunity for you."

She looked back, tears slipping a little faster down her cheeks. "It's not your choice to make, Noah."

"But it's my offer to rescind." He hated how much of a jerk he sounded like right now. Why did doing the thing he knew was best for the woman he loved have to feel so rotten? "I'm taking it back, Ev. I'm sorry." He pushed off the bed and hurried out the door before he caved.

CHAPTER 16

VERLY

"Merry Christmas, Mom!" Everly did her best to appear genuinely happy through the camera, but Mom's dropped smile meant she failed. "Kenobi," she called to the lab who was wandering the empty house since everyone was at Robyn's house for Christmas brunch. "Come say hi to Grandma Maureen."

"Everly, what's wrong?"

"Nothing. Nothing's wrong." It shouldn't be possible for tears to form anymore after how many of them she'd shed last night. "Did you and Aunt Suz make sticky rolls for breakfast?" she asked, wishing she had that one tradition to cling to this year. Sticky rolls made everything better.

"It's Noah, isn't it?"

Everly let out a heavy sigh, deciding it'd be futile to deny it. "You warned me. I didn't listen. End of story."

"Do you love him?"

Through a new flood of tears, Everly nodded. "I wish I didn't. It'd be easier."

"I wish I could give you a hug, hun."

"Me, too." She swiped at the tears with the sleeves of yesterday's sweater and struggled to pull herself together. "It's done, Mom. Let's talk about something else, okay?"

"Are you sure?"

"Yep. I'm sure." Everly'd spent too much time with her thoughts last night. Too much time to realize Noah must really love her if he didn't want her to give up her life in Snowy Falls. It was harder still to accept that he was right. How long would it take living on the ranch to resent him for what he asked her to give up? Six months? A year?

It's better this way.

"There's my granddog." Mom waved at Kenobi. The lab stared toward the window, searching for the owner of the voice. "Kenobi, look at the camera." Instead, he hopped his two front legs into Everly's lap and licked her cheek. "Ah, well, maybe next time," Mom said with a laugh. "Tell me all about your plans for your library and the New Year."

NOAH

"YOU'RE ALWAYS WELCOME BACK HOME," Mom said, hugging Noah tight enough to cut his oxygen supply. He didn't dare wriggle out of her grip until she was done, no matter how many of his siblings made faces from the living room window as if they were kids again. "Doesn't have to be for a holiday, either."

"I promise to visit more," Noah said for at least the fifth time today.

"It's noble what you're doing," Mom continued, following him to his truck as he lugged his suitcase along. "But I'm still mad at Arthur for putting that burden on you. He could've listed the entire Taggert family to take a turn before that unappreciative granddaughter of his."

"It is what it is." Shortly after spreading Arthur's ashes this morning, his entire family demanded an explanation of his new arrangement at the ranch. Already, three of his siblings made plans to visit. It should warm his heart that he finally felt like part of the family again. An emptiness lingered there instead.

"You love her, don't you? Chloe's friend?"

"Does *everyone* know?" he asked with a shaky laugh.

Mom softly patted his cheek. "Only everyone with eyes, dear."

Noah tossed his suitcase in the back seat of the truck and closed the door. "I wish I knew how to make it work. I guess it wasn't meant to be."

"You really believe that?" Mom challenged.

No. "I have to." Noah gave Mom one last hug and hopped into the truck. The eagerness he'd felt to leave on his first day in town was gone. Any urgency now was only to make his flight. "I'll be home for Easter," he promised.

"I'm counting on it."

Noah backed out of the driveway, forced to weave around cars that hadn't been there when he arrived days ago. With the sidewalks shoveled and the silhouettes of people passing by the living room window, everything finally felt normal again.

He hated to leave it all behind.

If only I could stay.

Goodbyes already exchanged with Grandma Annie this morning, he didn't dare stop by her house. The only way to ensure he held his ground and didn't allow Everly to sacrifice what she loved most was to avoid her.

His heart cracked open as he left the city limits, hoping and praying he'd made the right decision.

$\mathcal{N}$OAH

FALLING BACK into his old routine at Hope Valley was effortless. Within a week, Noah exhausted himself from dawn until dusk, catching up on all the duties he'd shirked while gone. Then there was Reed's ranch manager training list—all stipulations of Arthur's will.

But Noah liked the grueling pace. He *needed* the distraction. It was the only way to keep Everly a distant thought, as forgetting her was impossible.

"You eat too much pumpkin pie or something?" Reed ribbed after Noah dropped the wire cutters in the snow for the second time. "You constantly look like you've got a stomachache since you been back."

"Ate more than my fair share," Noah said without looking over. The less ammunition he gave Reed, the better. "Explain this whole fence repair thing one more time?"

"We can do this tomorrow," Reed offered. He held up the clipboard he carried whenever Noah was learning some new ranching task from Arthur's list. "You still have almost six months to get all this done."

"No, let's keep going."

Reed folded his arms and leaned against a fence post, shaking snow off the brim of his Stetson. Noah felt that assessing stare and plopped down on the snow-covered ground in defeat. If any other ranch hand were grading him on fence repair, Noah would force his way through the motions. But with Reed, it was pointless to try.

"You want to tell me what's really going on?" Reed pressed.

"Not really."

"What happened in Snowy Falls?"

"Nothing."

"Oh, geez." Reed clapped the wooden clipboard against his leg. "That means it's about a woman. Start talking."

"There's nothing to say."

"We can do this all day, Noah. You'll be frozen long before I will. Or you can cut right to the chase. What's her name?"

"Everly. Everly Jensen." Though Noah had zero

intentions of telling Reed or anyone else at the ranch about Everly, the moment her name escaped his lips, every detail of their time together poured with it. Including the reason Everly would never be happy long term at Hope Valley.

Reed studied him a minute longer than was comfortable, his eyebrows drawing together. "Why on earth did you come back *here*?"

Noah snapped his head up. "Why do you think? To protect everyone. I know what'll happen if Arthur's granddaughter gets a chance at the ranch."

Extending a hand, Reed pulled Noah to his feet. "So, you've met her?"

"Have you?" Noah asked.

"No. But Jed did. Says there's no way she'd last two weeks, much less a year, on this ranch. She has to do everything on this list first." Reed waved his clipboard at him before taking a seat in the UTV and waiting for Noah to do the same. "Did anyone tell you what happens if *she* fails?"

"No."

"The ranch remains in a trust. The two of you will have to make major decisions together, but selling it isn't an option after that. Not for thirty years."

Noah's heart thrummed in his chest as everything he thought he understood was slowly turned upside down. He didn't dare get his hopes up about a future with Everly, though. Not after the way he left things. "You'll get to stay on as manager?"

Reed flashed him a cheeky grin. "The two of you would have to vote unanimously to fire me or I stay. Didn't Arthur's lawyer explain any of this to you?"

"Guess not."

"Doesn't matter. There's only one task to worry about right now."

"What's that?"

"Packing your stuff so we can get you on the road first thing tomorrow morning."

"I can't go back. Not after the way I left things."

"Then grovel." Reed leveled with him a glare. "If you don't head out at daybreak tomorrow, I'll hog-tie you in the bed of my truck and drive you to Maine myself. I don't have to remind you that I still hold the state record for calf roping."

CHAPTER 18

EVERLY

EVERLY PEELED the last Christmas decoration from the wall in her library and hopped off the plastic stool. Two steps high and indoors she could manage, but she dreaded the day Annie requested the outdoor lights to come down.

Without the holiday cheer, Everly's library looked a little bland. But she had enough snowmen and snowflake decorations to fix that problem before school was back in session tomorrow. Why she put off coming here until the last minute wasn't something she could explain.

The library was her happy place, her escape.

Yet since Noah left town, Everly had avoided it

at all costs. She missed him a little more each day. His smile, his gentle way with animals, his kisses . . . maybe Everly was a fool to stay in Snowy Falls. But would she be a bigger fool to show up uninvited at Hope Valley?

"Any thoughts, Kenobi?" she asked her lounging lab. She could only bring him on non-school days, but today she was grateful for the company. He groaned a response, stretching and letting his eyes fall closed. "That's what I thought. Well, might as well get started."

She stared at the totes filled with winter décor and boxes stuffed with books for the New Year. Finding homes for them on her shelves would have to wait a few days. Rearranging the reading area would have to wait a few more.

"Need some help?"

Everly froze, convinced she was hearing things. Maybe if she stood really still, the voice would disappear and prove it was no more than her imagination. But Kenobi's collar jingled as he hopped to his feet. She heard the unmistakable thunk of his tail hitting her desk and was forced to turn around.

"Noah. You're . . . *here?*"

After an initial double-handed greeting with ear scratches and neck rubs—because they both knew Kenobi would have it no other way—Noah took slow, cautious steps toward her. "I'm here."

"Why? Is someone hurt, or—"

"No." He stopped a couple of feet from her and fiddled with the zipper on his jacket, letting out a nervous laugh. "I had all these things I wanted to say, and plenty of miles to figure them out. Would you believe I can't think of any of them?"

"I can't believe you're here." She took a half step forward, then held herself perfectly still, forcing out the question that needed answering. "How long?"

"To stay."

Everly's pulse doubled, then tripled. "You're moving home? What about Hope Valley and all those people depending on you to protect their livelihoods?"

"Turns out there's a loophole." Noah took another step closer and stopped. "They insisted I go so I wouldn't miss out on a lifetime with you." He reached out a hand, his fingertips brushing the edge of her cheek. "I'm in love with you, Everly Jensen. I have been for over four years. I wish I'd told you then, but I'm telling you now."

Heart melting and legs turning to noodles, Everly closed the gap between them. Falling into Noah's arms, she snaked both hands around his neck, pulling him a little closer as she went up on tiptoe. "You know what?"

"What?"

"I'm in love with you, too, Noah Taggert."

He swept her into a kiss that made the room spin and her heart soar higher than it ever had before.

This kiss promised a future together. One without distance or misunderstandings to unravel things. It promised happiness.

"I think it's time we tell your family about us," Everly said.

Noah kissed her once more. "Pretty sure they already have that figured out. But I guess I should let them know I'm back."

"You didn't tell them you were coming? *Again*?"

"What fun would that be?"

EPILOGUE

One year later...

ℕOAH

"BETTER HURRY UP." Noah dropped his hands on Everly's shoulders from behind the couch, rubbing her tight muscles. "Don't want to be late for the tree lighting."

"I'm only five pages from the end," Everly pleaded.

He kissed the top of her head, admiring the twinkling lights and carefully placed ornaments adorning their first Christmas tree. Everly picked this house

147

shortly after they were married because of the picture window in the living room. Not only could they display a big, fat tree, but Kenobi still had room to sit at the window without knocking into the ornaments.

"Did you think our first tree together would be this perfect?"

"Noah!"

Kissing her cheek this time, he moved away. "Okay, okay. I get the hint."

He gathered coats, gloves, scarves, and a leash, then waited for his wife to read the last sentence. As she did half the time when finishing a book, she threw the paperback down against the couch. Kenobi let out a bark. "Stupid cliffhangers. *Every* time."

Noah held out her coat and Everly slipped her arms into the sleeves. "At least you got out of the feast preparation at Grandma Annie's this year."

"Who drew the short straw anyway?"

"Blakely. She's convinced they rigged it to pay her back for the Cancun fiasco."

"She *would* think that."

"It might be true. Never know with us Taggerts." Noah clipped Kenobi's leash onto his collar and held out his hand to Everly. "Ready for our big announcement tonight?"

Everly rubbed her tiny baby bump, glowing with happiness. "I bet half of them already have it figured out."

"Want to put a wager on that?" Noah teased.

"Don't you still owe me twenty dollars from last Christmas?"

Noah kissed her on the cheek. "I don't know what you're talking about."

SWEET ROMANCE

Sunset Ridge Series
    1 - Moose Be Love
    2 - My Favorite Moosetake
    3 - Annoymoosely Yours
    4 - Love & Moosechief
    5 - Under the Mooseltoe

Starlight Cowboys Series
    1 - Cowboys & Starlight
    2 - Cowboys & Firelight
    3 - Cowboys & Sunrises
    4 - Cowboys & Moonlight
    5 - Cowboys & Mistletoe
    6 - Cowboys & Shooting Stars

Stand-Alone
  *Hooked on You

Christmas in Snowy Falls
  *Pawsitively in Love Again at Christmas
  *Pawsitively Home for Christmas

STEAMY ROMANTIC SUSPENSE

Willow Creek Series
  1 - Sweetly Scandalous
  2 - Secretly Scandalous
  3 - Simply Scandalous

Sign up for Jacqueline Winter's newsletter to receive alerts about current projects and new releases!

http://eepurl.com/du18iz

ABOUT THE AUTHOR

Jacqueline Winters has been writing since she was nine when she'd sneak stacks of paper from her grandma's closet and fill them with adventure. She grew up in small-town Nebraska and spent a decade living in beautiful Alaska. She writes sweet contemporary romance and contemporary romantic suspense.

She's a sucker for happily ever after's, has a sweet tooth that can be sated with cupcakes. On a relaxing evening, you can find her at her computer writing her next novel with her faithful dog poking his adorable nose over her keyboard.

Made in the USA
Monee, IL
21 October 2020

45724486R00100